COMA
'WHAT IF' I NEVER BECAME A NAVY SEAL?

By

Jason D White

Speculative Memoir

Psychological Thriller

Table of Contents

The taste of copper filled my mouth as consciousness clawed its way back. My training demanded I catalogue threats—location, exits, hostiles—but my body betrayed me. Even my eyelids felt foreign, heavy as blast doors.

"Can you hear me? You've been in a coma for a year."

A year. The word echoed in the hollow space where my mind should have been sharp, where my situational awareness should have been flawless. A year of my life, gone. In my world, a second's hesitation meant death. A year was an eternity.

I forced my eyes open, expecting the crisp clarity that had kept me alive through two decades of warfare. Instead, the world swam in soft focus—a weakness I couldn't afford. The figure beside my bed was a blur in white, probably a doctor, definitely not a threat. But in that moment of vulnerability, I needed to remember who I was. I needed to rebuild myself from the inside out.

"Listen carefully," I said, my voice scraping like sandpaper. "I am Jason the MONSTER. Military Operations Navy SEAL Trained Elite Recon. I am not a monster to the innocent, but to my enemy—do not become my enemy."

The words felt like armor sliding back into place. "I have a kill count of approximately 76 souls, all in service to this country. I have served under four US presidents, shaken their hands, earned their trust. I wear my trident with pride, backed by the Meritorious Service Medal and the Legion of Merit."

My mind traveled beyond these sterile walls, to mountains in Afghanistan, jungles in South America, frozen tundra in Alaska. "My feet have touched all seven continents, my body has cut through all five seas, my lungs have breathed the air of all fifty states. I have literally been around the world."

But even as I spoke these truths, a different truth gnawed at me. Before the military found me, I was nothing—a directionless kid who became a misguided teenager, wasting away because I had given up on myself. Twenty years I gave to the service: three years of the hardest training on Earth, ten years as an active SEAL, seven more in the reserves. In return, they gave me purpose, discipline, and brotherhood. They gave me a reason to exist.

Throughout those years, lying in my bunk between missions, I would sometimes wonder: What if I'd never listened to Rivera? What if I'd never become a Navy SEAL? What kind of man would I have become?

Now, staring at the ceiling of this hospital room, tubes snaking from my arms like mechanical veins, that question felt more urgent than ever. A year of my life had vanished. A year where anything could have happened, where I could have been anyone. It made me wonder about all the other paths I'd never taken, all the other versions of myself that might have existed.

The military had saved me from a life of nothing. But as I lay there, suspended between who I was and who I'd been, one question haunted me more than any mission briefing I've ever had.

What if I never became a Navy SEAL?

Until, one day, I actually found out.

CHAPTER 1

Why Do I Have To Go To The Military?

"When you turn eighteen, you're going to the military."

My mother delivered this decree with the same certainty she used to announce dinner or bedtime. There was no room for discussion, no hint that this might be a choice. It was simply my fate, as inevitable as growing taller or losing teeth.

The weight of this predetermined future followed me everywhere, even to the park where my cousin Mike and I were engaged in the serious business of burying a sock. We were seven, maybe eight, and the military loomed in my mind like a storm cloud on a distant horizon.

"What branch are you planning on joining when you go to the military?" I asked him, patting down the dirt over our buried treasure.

Mike looked at me like I'd asked what color the sky was on Mars. "I'm not going to no military. My parents never said I had to go."

The confusion hit me like a physical blow. Why did he get to choose while I was already enlisted in my mother's mind? His father, my Uncle Mike, was the tougher, no-nonsense guy—you'd think he'd be the one pushing military service. But somehow, Mike got to be a regular kid with a regular future while I was marked for something I didn't understand.

We moved on to more pressing matters— Egg McMuffins —but the question lingered. Why was I different? Maybe it was because Mike was always so bright and had the option to go to college, while for someone like me, the military felt like the only real path. That was the only way my younger self could make sense of it all.

School only reinforced that feeling. While I was quick with my schoolwork and caught on faster than most kids, the teachers saw something else entirely. They saw a problem that needed fixing.

"Jason has ADD," they told my mother, as if they'd discovered some hidden defect. "He needs medication to help him focus."

Just like that, I became the kid who had to take his "crazy medicine" in the middle of class. Ritalin. A little pill that was supposed to "calm me down," make me more manageable. The other kids made sure I never forgot I was different, their taunts following me to the nurse's office every day.

But here's what they didn't understand: I wasn't struggling because I couldn't learn. I was bored because I already knew the material. Every afternoon, my grandmother would sit with me at our dining room table, teaching me things the school wouldn't cover for months. She was my secret weapon, my academic advantage, and my strongest advocate.

"That boy doesn't have ADD," she'd tell my mother firmly. "He's just as normal as any other kid."

Grandma saw through the diagnosis, understood that a child being a child wasn't a medical condition. While the school wanted to drug me into compliance, she wanted to challenge me, to feed my curiosity instead of suppressing it. Thanks to her, I excelled academically despite the label they'd stuck on me.

The irony wasn't lost on me even then. If I truly needed this medication to function, why did I only take it at school? At home, I was perfectly normal—no pills required. For nine months of the year, they pumped me full of what I'd later learn was a Schedule II controlled substance, the same classification as cocaine. Then, for three months of summer vacation, I was magically cured.

Everything changed in 1994. Sixth grade. Grandma passed away, and with her went my anchor, my advocate, my reason to care about anything. I shut down completely. The homework went undone, the classwork ignored. School, which had once been easy despite its challenges, became meaningless.

Without Grandma's influence, my mother took me off the Ritalin cold turkey. Years of daily medication, stopped overnight. No weaning, no gradual reduction, just an abrupt end to a chemical dependency I'd developed as a child. The withdrawal was brutal, though no one seemed to notice or care.

For the first time in my academic career, I failed. Sixth grade became a prison sentence I couldn't escape, a year that stretched endlessly as I watched my classmates move on while I remained stuck. The failure felt like proof of everything the school had said about me—that I was broken, different, unable to succeed without their intervention.

The isolation was complete. Without Grandma's daily support, I had no one. My mother worked, my teachers saw me as a problem case, and my classmates had moved on to seventh grade. A twelve-year-old boy who'd just lost the most important person in his life was left to figure out why he was suddenly failing at everything.

Nobody asked why. Nobody wondered if grief might explain the dramatic change in a child who'd been successful for years. Instead, they labeled me a failure and moved on.

The comparison to my cousin Lil Kenny was impossible to ignore. He was just as mischievous as I'd been, just as energetic, just as likely to crack jokes when he should have been paying attention. But he roamed the halls pill-free and unjudged and nobody ever suggested he had a learning disability. Nobody forced medication down his throat. He got to be a normal kid while I was made to believe something was fundamentally wrong with me. Why was I the only one made to feel broken?

The questions multiplied in my mind, each one more urgent than the last. Why was I treated differently? Why did I have to take medication that made me feel like a zombie? Why did everyone seem to think I was sick when I felt perfectly fine?

And underneath it all, the biggest question of all—the one that would follow me for years to come:

Why do I have to go to the military?

CHAPTER 2

My New Home Away From Home

The teenage years hit me like a tidal wave. Suddenly, I was an expert on everything, a know-it-all in a world that refused to bend to my will. My newfound wisdom, however, rarely extended to my schoolwork, a fact that wore on my mother's last nerve. Her warnings began to shift. The familiar refrain of my childhood, the one about the military, was replaced with a new set of ultimatums.

"When you turn eighteen, you're moving out of my house."

"When you turn eighteen, you can do whatever you want to do."

The change was jarring. For years, my future had been a fixed point, a military uniform hanging in a closet I hadn't yet seen. Now, she was handing me a blank map. The contradiction gnawed at me until I finally had to confront it.

"Mom," I asked one afternoon, the words tumbling out in a rush of confusion, "You spent my whole childhood telling me the military was my only choice. Now you're saying I can do whatever I want? I found out it's not mandatory. Why did you make it sound like I had no other option?"

She paused, her gaze softening, surprised that I even remembered that. For the first time, I saw not just a disciplinarian, but a single mother grappling with a difficult reality. "I told you that," she began, her voice quiet, "because I *wanted* it for you. You're my oldest, and unlike your cousins, you don't have a man in the house to teach you how to be one. I can't teach you that. I figured the military... it could give you things I never could. It could teach you structure, discipline. It could take you places I'll never be able to show you."

Her words landed with a surprising weight. It made a strange kind of sense, a desperate plan born from a mother's love and fear. But even as I understood her reasoning, a defiant part of me dug its heels in. *I'm definitely not joining the military,* I thought, *especially if I don't have to.* The revelation that it was a choice, not a command, felt like a get-out-of-jail-free card. I was passing on that future.

My high school years, however, proved that my own plans weren't leading me anywhere promising. I spent three years, from 1996 to 1999, drifting through the halls of Woodward High School, a place with a long history in Cincinnati. By the time I reached the ninth grade, I was so far behind that the school and my mom decided on a drastic change. I was placed in a split-day program: half a day of classes, and the other half on a job hunt. That's how I landed my first real gig, slinging burgers at McDonald's in 1998.

At McDonald's, I worked alongside kids from Aiken High School. In my mind, a change of scenery seemed like the magic bullet for my academic woes. I convinced my mom that a transfer to Aiken would be the fresh start I needed. Desperate for any sign of progress, she moved mountains to make it happen. But a new school didn't mean a new me. I was failing just as quickly at Aiken as I had at Woodward.

One small change from that time did stick. My eyesight had always been terrible, a fact I'd tried to ignore since elementary school by "accidentally" breaking every pair of nerdy glasses I was given. But in the fluorescent lights of high school classrooms, I could no longer deny the blur. I finally gave in and got contact lenses. With lenses in place, the hallways sharpened into focus—but my grades stayed blurry. At least I could see the assignments I was failing.

With my high school career circling the drain, my mom played her last card. Graduation was a fantasy, a finish line I had no hope of reaching. She had to face the harsh truth, as she watched everyone else celebrate their kids graduating from high school, she knew that would not be a reality for her oldest son. So, she decided to pull me out of the public school system altogether and enroll me in Job Corps.

Job Corps, she explained, was a residential program where people from 17 to 24 could earn a GED and learn a trade. It was her last hope, a final, desperate attempt to set me on a path that didn't lead to a dead end. The program offered training in everything from culinary arts and carpentry to auto mechanics and welding.

"You should take up welding," my mom suggested, her voice filled with a fragile optimism. "Your Uncle Mike does it, and he makes good money."

I didn't have a passion for welding, or for any of the other trades for that matter. I was a ship without a rudder, and at that point, I was willing to let someone else take the helm. I chose welding, not because I wanted it, but because she did. I packed my bags, ready to trade my failing high school career for a GED and a trade. I was headed to Cincinnati Job Corps,

my new home away from home.

CHAPTER 3

I Got It From Here

Job Corps was just a different-colored high school when I first arrived in October 2000. I brought the same apathy, the same lack of direction that had defined my teenage years. But something about the place—a melting pot of people from Cincinnati, Detroit, Chicago, and beyond—began to slowly chip away at my indifference. My mom had insisted I live on campus even though we were from the same city, wanting me to be fully immersed in the experience. It worked.

I made friends quickly, including my roommate Wyvon. We arrived on the same day, two Cincinnati boys stepping into a new world together. But there was a key difference between us that became clear immediately. Wyvon already had his high school diploma; he was at Job Corps with a clear plan—to get a culinary degree and build a career. I was just there, a piece of driftwood caught in a current my mother had chosen for me.

The current changed one afternoon in my welding class. A friend named Rivera started talking about a meeting he had scheduled with a Navy recruiter. I barely paid him any mind until he said the words that would alter the course of my life forever.

"I'm going to be a Navy SEAL," he said, and the way he said it—with a fire and passion I'd never seen in anyone—made me stop what I was doing and listen. He spoke of them as if they were modern-day Spartans, the most elite warriors on the planet. "Hey," he said, turning to me with eyes lit with excitement, "maybe you should do it too."

I brushed it off immediately. "Nah, I'm good."

But Rivera was persistent, less like a friend making a suggestion and more like a missionary who had found his calling. He wasn't selling me on the Navy; he was selling me on the man I could become. You would've thought he was a recruiter himself, the way he talked about the training, the brotherhood, the purpose. I left him that day telling him no, but the seed was planted.

I thought about it. Then I thought about it some more. And the more I pictured it—me, a Navy SEAL—the more the idea took root and grew from a casual thought into a full-blown obsession. I started hanging out with Rivera exclusively. We'd work out together, our conversations circling constantly around training, missions, and the unbreakable will of a SEAL. This wasn't just a whim anymore. This was a purpose I'd never felt before.

I remembered my mom's words from years ago, her desperate wish for the military to make me the man she couldn't teach me to be. I thought about how no one in our family had ever served. I would be the first. The idea solidified in my mind, hardening from something I wanted to do into something I had to do.

I started making the calls, announcing my new life plan to family and friends. Most were thrilled, if a little bewildered by the sudden transformation. But the first real pushback came from two people I had only just gotten to know: my older brothers.

I was my mom's oldest, but on my dad's side, I had four other siblings I'd only met that year at eighteen. When I told my oldest brother, Nate, his reaction cut deep. "We just met, man," he said, his voice heavy with disappointment. "We missed our whole childhood together. Now you're gonna leave again?" He quoted a line from Boyz n the Hood that stuck with me: "There's no place for a black man in a white man's army."

My second older brother, Donnie, was actively serving in the Air Force and trying to get out. His reasons were more pragmatic but equally discouraging. "You don't want to be in the military with George Bush in office," he warned. "And the Navy? You'll spend months on a ship in the middle of the ocean with nothing but dudes."

"I'm not just joining the Navy," I argued, feeling my resolve strengthen against his resistance. "I'm going to be a SEAL. That's completely different."

Nothing they said could deter me. Seeing my unwavering determination, Donnie's tone eventually softened. He didn't like my choice, but he became supportive. When I finally told my mom, she just shook her head and smiled with that look she got when she was both proud and worried. "A Navy SEAL? Wow. It takes twenty years to become a SEAL." It was her classic exaggeration, but beneath it, I could see she was proud that her boy had finally found something worth fighting for.

The first real test came when Rivera went to meet his recruiter. I tagged along, and the recruiter had me take a preliminary exam—a practice ASVAB to see where I stood academically. As I finished, another man in the office, someone I'd never seen before, snatched my test sheet without introduction. He looked me up and down with an air of pure disdain.

"Yeah, he ain't ready," he sneered to the recruiter, talking about me like I wasn't sitting right there. "I can see he's not cut out for this." He scanned my answers with theatrical disgust. "I can look at one question and know if he's got it or not." His finger landed on a specific line. "Yep. Like I said. Not ready."

The question was a classic ethics-versus-orders dilemma: You are stationed in a lighthouse with strict orders not to leave your post. A boat capsizes nearby, and the injured survivors call for help. What do you do? I had chosen the answer that seemed obvious to me: Go to the boat and help the people.

"If your orders are to stay in the lighthouse," the man said, his voice dripping with condescension, "why would you disobey a direct order?"

The recruiter just watched, letting the humiliation sink in, as if this public degradation was part of the process. The sting of that moment, of being made to feel stupid and unfit in front of strangers, ignited something in me I didn't know existed. The recruiter finally stepped in with a more reasonable tone.

"Look," he said calmly, "we can work on that. But first, you have to get your GED. You can't enlist without it. Second… you wear contacts, right?"

I nodded.

"That's a problem for the SEALs," he explained matter-of-factly. He told me about the risk of infection, of a lens dislodging during a critical underwater mission. "If you're serious about this path, you need to look into LASIK eye surgery. It's not a requirement for the regular Navy, though. You're taking welding at Job Corps, right? The Navy needs welders. It's a good career. Something to think about."

Now I had a choice. A safe path as a Navy welder, or a risky, expensive surgery for a shot at the only thing I now wanted. There was no dilemma in my mind. I was going to be a SEAL.

I told Wyvon my plan when I got back to our room. "Why would you want to do that?" he asked, genuinely confused by my sudden intensity.

I turned the question on him. "You've got your diploma. Why are you here?"

"To get my culinary degree," he said, as if it were the most obvious thing in the world.

"Exactly," I shot back. "You came here with a plan. I didn't. My mom brought me here because I was failing at everything else. But now, I have a plan. I have a reason to finish this place and start my life."

He nodded slowly, understanding dawning on his face. "Okay, I feel you on that. That's what's up. But a Navy SEAL, though… you sure you're gonna be ready for that kind of intensity?"

"Man," I said, looking him dead in the eye, "I hope so. Because I don't have any other plans."

On June 5th, 2001, I failed my first attempt at the GED by a handful of points. Reality hit hard. This piece of paper was the first wall between me and my future, and I had just run straight into it. My resolve hardened like steel. I buried myself in books, studying every day with the same intensity I planned to bring to SEAL training.

One day, I was sitting in one of my classes, half-listening to the lesson because I had a lot on my mind, when the teacher suddenly turned on me. Her voice cut through the room like a blade. "Are you even paying attention? Or are you just going to sit there looking lost as usual?"

The words hit me like a freight train. That familiar knot of shame twisted in my chest—suddenly I was eight years old again, listening to whispers about the "slow kid" who needed extra help.

"Can you even follow what we're discussing?" Her voice grew sharper, more condescending. Every pair of eyes in the room turned toward me. "Because if you were paying attention, you wouldn't be looking lost… Duh."

Whenever someone ends their sentence with "Duh", they are, in some way, saying that you are dumb.

Heat flooded my face. My hands clenched into fists. Every instinct screamed at me to unleash the fury building in my throat, to tell her exactly what I thought of her attitude. The words were right there, burning on my tongue.

Instead, I pushed back my chair with a sharp scrape. The sound echoed through the suddenly silent classroom as I stood up and walked toward the door. I needed to cool down before I did something that would prove every assumption she'd ever made about me or that I might later regret. Besides, I'd rather get in trouble for walking out of class than cussing her out and getting kicked out of

Job Corps.

The oppressive heat of August in Cincinnati always signaled one major thing: the Midwest Black Family Reunion. My friend Wyvon, an eternal enthusiast for any massive social gathering, had been hyping it up for weeks. Despite the looming cloud of the GED test—a date that was creeping closer on the calendar—I knew I couldn't pass up the opportunity. Besides, my study habits were strictly a school-hours affair; weekends and summer nights were for living.

We arrived to a roar of music, sizzling food from countless vendors, and a sea of people that stretched across the park. The energy was infectious. Wyvon, with his magnetic personality, quickly linked up with a small crew of guys he knew. Among them was Rico, who had the easy confidence of someone who was intimately familiar with the city's social scene.

The objective of the day, as it was for most teenage guys at an event like this, quickly boiled down to a single, competitive sport: collecting phone numbers. Wyvon treated it like a high-stakes scavenger hunt, moving from group to group with practiced ease. Initially, I hung back, content to just soak in the atmosphere. "Just chillin'," was my internal mantra. But after watching Wyvon rack up a small stack of scribbled paper, the competitive urge finally kicked in. I was notoriously shy when it came to approaching girls I didn't know, but after that initial, awkward first attempt, a surprising wave of confidence washed over me. It was a numbers game, and I was finally in it.

We were making our way past a row of seating areas when I stopped dead. I nudged Wyvon and simply pointed. The girl sitting there—her profile caught by the afternoon sun—was captivating. Before Wyvon could even look, Rico's voice cut in, laced with a cynical familiarity.

"Yea, I know her," Rico stated, shaking his head. "She be giving niggas the wrong number. You can try if you want to, though."

Rico's casual dismissal did more than just relay a warning; it lit a fuse. I hadn't even fully decided to approach her yet, but his comment instantly transformed the interaction from a simple flirtation into a direct challenge to my newfound confidence.

"Is that right?" I thought, a mischievous grin spreading across my face.

I walked over with a deliberate stride, took the empty space next to her, and smoothly initiated a conversation. I don't remember exactly what I said—probably some combination of event commentary and a compliment—but I recall her laughing easily. When the conversation wound down, she asked for my phone, but then paused, pulled out her own pen, and wrote a number down on a scrap of paper instead.

Triumphantly, I walked back and shoved the paper into Rico's face. He snatched it, scanning the digits before looking up at me, a flicker of genuine surprise in his eyes.

"Damn," he admitted. "She must *really* like you, man. That's the right number."

I met his gaze and confidently shot back the only appropriate response: "Oh, you thought it wasn't going to be?" The small victory over Rico's skepticism felt almost as good as getting the number itself.

A day or two later, the flurry of the reunion had settled, and I was going through the collection of numbers I'd amassed. I stopped when I reached hers—Shana. The name was as unique as her presence had been. I dialed the number, my stomach doing a slight flip.

"Hello?" a voice answered.

"Hey, can I speak to Shana?"

"This her, who is this?"

"This is Jason. We met at the Black Family Reunion."

There was a slight pause, and then recognition clicked in her voice. "Oh, hey, Jason!" she said. But then her tone shifted, becoming playfully serious. She asked a question I had absolutely never been asked before:

"How many numbers did you get that day?"

I froze. My mind raced. Should I lie? Say she was the only one? No, that would be transparently false and disrespectful to the context of the event. I'd decided earlier to keep it real with myself, and I decided to keep it real with her.

"Seven," I admitted, trying to sound nonchalant.

"Seven?" she repeated, a slight edge in her voice. "You got seven numbers that day?"

"Y-yea," I stammered, instantly regretting my honesty and bracing for a reaction.

Then came the punchline, delivered with blunt, perfect timing.

"Nigga, you got six too many," she declared, and hung up.

I stood there, receiver in hand, completely stunned for a beat. There was no way she was serious. It had to be a test. A joke. Grinning, I immediately hit the redial button. It barely rang once before she answered.

"Nigga, ain't nobody tell you to call me right back," she said, but this time, I could hear the unmistakable sound of laughter bubbling up in her voice.

"You knew I was going to call back," I countered, feeling relieved. "The phone barely rang before you answered it."

I don't know if she had strategized that move, but it was brilliant. In two quick sentences and one abrupt hang-up, Shana hadn't just given me a number; she had established a dominant, unforgettable tone. She immediately stood out from every other girl I'd met that day. The truth was, after that call, the other six numbers became completely irrelevant. I don't think I ever even bothered to call the rest of them.

I was scheduled to retake the test on September 11, 2001. After the test, I went to my little cousin Jalen's third birthday party. When I got back to Job Corps that afternoon, the world had changed.

Everyone was clustered around TVs, talking about a terrorist attack in New York, about planes and the Twin Towers. I honestly didn't know what to make of it. The only thing consuming my mind was whether or not I had passed that test.

A week later, I got the results. PASSED. A wave of relief and confidence washed over me like nothing I'd ever experienced. I still had to finish the welding program—my Plan B—and completing it would give me a cash bonus I desperately needed. My focus narrowed to two things: finishing welding and crushing the ASVAB.

The final obstacle was money. LASIK was going to cost $2,700. The bonus for completing Job Corps was only $1,500. It felt insurmountable, but while I was grinding through my studies, my mom was working her own magic behind the scenes.

In April 2002, I finished the welding program and took the ASVAB. I didn't just pass; I scored high enough for both a welding job and consideration for SEAL training. The confidence from passing the GED had propelled me forward like rocket fuel. Rivera had already left for the Navy by then. The guy who had started me on this path was gone, and I could only hope our paths would cross again somewhere down the line.

My graduation from Job Corps was in May. The very next day, I went in for my LASIK appointment. I spent a few weeks recovering to ensure my eyes were fully healed, and then I shipped out for the Navy. Everything was finally falling into place with military precision.

After the graduation, the whole family gathered at my Uncle Kenny's house. This wasn't just a graduation party; it was a going-away party, a celebration of transformation. For years, I'd been a guest at these celebrations for others—cousins graduating and achieving milestones. Now, I was the reason we were all here.

One by one, my family members took the microphone to offer congratulations. My mom spoke of her pride, her voice thick with emotion. My aunts and uncles shared their own words of encouragement and amazement at my turnaround. Then, my Uncle Mike took the mic. He congratulated me, and then he looked right at me and said something that changed everything.

His gift, he announced, was to pay for my LASIK surgery. In full. He spoke of how hard my mom had been working to scrape the money together and said he wanted me to start my journey without that financial burden weighing me down.

In that single moment, everything crystallized. My entire life, every wrong turn and every small victory, had been shaped by the quiet, relentless force of my mother's love and my family's support. She had put me in a school that labeled me, then fought for me when I needed an advocate. She had pushed me toward a military I resented, only for me to find my own way there. She had sent me to Job Corps when I was failing at everything else, and that's where I finally found a dream worth chasing.

Though I hated public speaking, I knew I had to say something. I walked to the front, took the microphone with trembling hands, and thanked everyone for their generosity. Then, I turned to my mom.

"You know," I began, my voice thick with emotion I couldn't hide, "I never realized how much you guided me to this point. You did everything you could to keep me from sinking. When I was failing at Woodward, you put me in Aiken upon my request, then sent me to Job Corps when that didn't work out. You got me this far." I looked out at the faces of my family, then back at the woman who had never given up on me, even when I had given up on myself. Then I said with stern confidence,

"I got it from here."

CHAPTER 4

That Was Just The Beginning

Shana and I had grown incredibly close over the past 9 months. In the whirlwind of late nights studying, shared laughter, and quiet, meaningful conversations, she had become an integral part of my life. Trust had blossomed into something deeper, and with that closeness came the difficult obligation to share my long-held ambition: my plan to join the Navy and train to become a SEAL.

I remember the conversation vividly. We were at our usual meet up spot, Fountain Square, the air thick with the promise of summer. I laid out my future, emphasizing the demanding nature of the training and the inevitable, long periods of distance the military life would require. My voice was weighted with uncertainty as I spoke about the practical realities—how a relationship, especially one so new and with us both being so young, could possibly weather the kind of separation and inherent risk that path entailed. It felt unfair to ask her to wait, or to commit to something so uncertain.

We talked for hours, our youthful optimism clashing with the harsh logistics of my chosen career. The decision was painful but mutual: we couldn't proceed as a couple, not with this enormous, immovable obstacle looming. We knew that as soon as I shipped out, everything would change.

And then, that time arrived. The orders were cut, the date was set, and the reality of my departure became immediate. With a heavy heart, and a painful recognition of what had to be done for both our futures, Shana and I had to break things off. It was the hardest farewell, a necessary severance that marked the beginning of my new life and the end of the beautiful chapter we had shared.

I grabbed her hand, the contact immediate and electric even through the thin fabric of her coat sleeve. A desperate, final thought spilled from my lips, a flimsy promise against the crushing weight of the present moment. "You know," I began, my voice a little rougher than I intended, my eyes searching hers for some anchor of hope, "maybe we'll see each other again in the future."

The word 'future' hung between us, a vast, unreachable chasm. To her, a young woman steeped in farewells, the promise felt like an empty, well-meaning lie designed to soften a permanent separation. Her gaze, steady with haunting resignation, made my heart ache. She didn't recoil or argue, but offered a reply more profound and final than my optimistic half-truth.

Lifting her chin, a faint, melancholy smile touching her lips, she replied in a whisper against the traffic's hum, "Or maybe in another life.

In that single, breathtaking sentence, she acknowledged the impossibility of the present, the unlikelihood of any *future* reunion, and the deep, inescapable connection that bound us—a bond so absolute that it transcended this brief, fleeting existence. It was a beautiful, devastating form of acceptance, a quiet understanding that our story was over in *this* world, leaving only the hope of an impossible, cosmic reunion.

I remembered standing in the kitchen years earlier, questioning my mom about the military. One of her reasons, she'd said, was that the military could take me places she never could. Now, here it was. The first of those places was Great Lakes, Illinois—home of Naval Station Great Lakes, the boot camp for every sailor in the United States Navy.

Before this, my world had been impossibly small. Outside the tri-state area of Ohio, Kentucky, and Indiana, I'd only ever been to Panama City and Atlanta, both times as a kid tagging along with my cousin Mike's family and Detroit Michigan with my mom, and her boyfriend, Dan at the time in '96. Now, I was stepping onto a path that would be defined by travel—a life lived out of a sea bag.

With vision sharpened by LASIK surgery that felt like a metaphor for my entire existence, I could finally see my future clearly. That afternoon, I packed my duffel bag under the watchful eyes of my mom and little brother Kenny. I hugged my mom, kissing her cheek, then turned to shake Kenny's hand.

He bypassed it completely.

Instead, he pulled me into a hug that caught me off guard—the warmest, tightest embrace I'd ever felt from him. He gripped my shoulders, forcing me to meet his gaze. "I'm proud of you, bro," he said simply. "You came a long way."

In that instant, I understood he had been watching me all along. This was the brother I'd shared a room with, the one with whom I'd invented games and inside jokes that belonged only to us. He was my first best friend. He'd seen the light go out in me when our grandmother died. He'd witnessed my struggle through high school—the slow-motion self-destruction. For years, I had been a living example of what *not* to become.

That hug wasn't just goodbye. It was gratitude. A silent acknowledgment that I had finally given him a different example to follow. *I knew you had it in you,* it seemed to say. *Now go make us all proud.*

I traded my Job Corps ID for a series of physicals and examinations at the Military Entrance Processing Station. As the bus finally pulled away, carrying me toward the most profound change of my life, a hush fell over my thoughts. I was leaving everything behind.

Damn, I thought, the words echoing in the quiet of my mind. *I'm really doing this.*

The roar of the bus engine gave way to the sharp, salty air of Naval Station Great Lakes. Diesel fumes mixed with the metallic scream of drills. My sea bag thudded against concrete—the first sound of a life stripped to its essentials. I looked at the hundred other recruits, their faces mixing fear with forced bravado, and felt my own heart hammering against my ribs.

The experience of processing vanished in a dazzle of bright overhead lights, antiseptic tastes, and vaccination stings. We surrendered every scrap of our civilian identities—clothes, pictures, even our names. We were reborn as numbers, stenciled onto crisp new uniforms. The voices of our Recruit Division Commanders became a constant, barking torrent of standards: haircuts, uniform wear, watch standing. There was no hiding. No slipping through cracks.

The first week brought swim qualification. The cap squeezed my skull and cold water shocked my system. They drilled us on breaststroke, sidestroke, and the dreaded drown-proofing exercise. The pool—once a symbol of summer fun and lazy afternoons—had become a laboratory of controlled drowning. Carefree laughter was replaced by sharp instructor barks and desperate recruit gasps. This wasn't fun. It was survival, pure and brutal.

Passing that test tasted sweeter than any victory I'd ever known.

Being in that water dredged up a memory, leading to a startling realization: I was lucky I already knew how to swim. Or rather, that I had discovered I could.

I met my best friend Ya-Cob in third grade. During summers, I'd stay at his house and we'd go to Chase Pool. The first time we went, all the kids were talking about jumping off the high dive into the twelve-foot deep end. I'd never been in water over my head. Admitting I couldn't swim wasn't an option.

As the line moved forward, I watched carefully, studying how other kids hit the water. They'd splash down, then with simple waves of arms and legs, just... float. They made it look as easy as breathing.

When my turn came, I stood on the board, heart pounding. There was no turning back.

I jumped.

Water enveloped me. Then instinct took over. I kicked my legs, moved my arms, and just like the others, I swam away as if I'd been doing it my whole life. It was easier than riding a bike. I couldn't understand how anyone could drown.

Yet here, in Navy boot camp pools, men who had willingly joined a maritime service were terrified of water. Some couldn't swim a single stroke. It baffled me, but I didn't judge. I knew that somewhere down the line, I would find my own high dive—my own moment of truth where I was the one completely lost.

Seeing I had a skill others lacked gave me a quiet flicker of confidence. For the first time, maybe I wasn't the one playing catch-up.

Physical training was relentless. Mornings began at 0500 with three-mile runs through pre-dawn fog and muscle-shredding calisthenics. We hauled heavy logs in perfect unison—the price of failure being more push-ups, more flutter kicks, more pain. Every blister and aching muscle reminded me I was being broken down and rebuilt. The person I used to be was vanishing, one painful repetition at a time.

Afternoons meant classroom time: learning ancient Navy customs, damage control, firefighting. We learned to tie knots that could secure warships and battled controlled fires with roaring hoses. Burnt rubber and boot leather became the new scents of my life.

Then came the Confidence Course—a twisted version of a childhood playground. A suspended gauntlet of cargo nets, ropes, and narrow beams forty feet above ground. I thought about when I was a kid scrambling over jungle gyms for fun, my laughter echoing through parks. There was no laughter here. This wasn't a game but a grueling test of will, designed to push us to breaking points.

My legs shook as I ascended the first net, wind whipping at my uniform. Every step was a battle between fear and trust—trust in the harness, trust in myself. At the end, we took a controlled plunge into safety nets. The scream that tore from my lungs transformed into laughter of pure, unadulterated triumph.

The final test was a forty-eight-hour crucible of night navigation, patrol simulations, and sleep-deprived problem-solving. We huddled behind sandbags, planned missions by flashlight, and were woken at all hours for inspections. We were grimy, exhausted, running on fumes.

But we finished.

I called my mom and told her to gather the family for graduation. To my astonishment, they came in force: my dad, my brothers Nate and Donnie, my sisters Kisha and Crystal—everyone. Just months earlier, they had all traveled to Columbus to watch my cousin Lil Kenny play in a basketball tournament. Now they were all in Illinois. For me.

On graduation morning, we stood at attention in pressed dress blues, white hats gleaming under the sun. As I marched past the stands, my family's faces a proud, emotional blur, I felt the weight of tradition settle on my shoulders.

I understood then that this ceremony wasn't an ending.

That was just the beginning.

CHAPTER 5

Jason The MONSTER is Born

The bus ride to Illinois had been the first step. Boarding the plane to California was a leap into another dimension. It was my first time on an airplane, and as we crossed time zones, the world I knew literally fell away behind me. I was heading west, farther than I'd ever been, to the coast of the Pacific Ocean—where boys were broken and SEALs were forged.

Before dawn, the bus rolled onto Naval Amphibious Base Coronado. Through windows misted with breath and nerves, I saw them: the instructors, prowling the "grinder" like wolves eyeing fresh prey. This wasn't boot camp. This was BUD/S. This was where everything would be stripped away.

Class 260. That number gave me comfort. It was my moms birthday. February of 1960.

The first two weeks—"Indoc"—were deceptively calm. We learned the compound, the rhythm of physical training, and the unspoken rules of a world where weakness was fatal. Assigned to Boat Crew 2, I found myself in the middle of the pack: neither the strongest nor the weakest, just another candidate grimly determined to endure.

Then Phase 1 struck like a sledgehammer.

Mornings began with surf torture—locking arms with my boat crew as the icy Pacific crashed over us, cold cutting deeper than any physical blow. We ran for miles on soft, energy-sapping sand. We swam until our limbs went numb. We did push-ups until our knuckles bled on concrete. Back at Job Corps, Rivera and I had talked a big game, but we could never have imagined brutality like this. I thought I was ready.

I wasn't.

Some pain, you just have to survive.

The hardest part wasn't the physical agony—it was the doubt. In the dead of night, soaked to the bone and shivering uncontrollably, exhaustion became a voice in my head. A seductive whisper telling me to quit. *That welding job in the Navy doesn't sound so bad right about now.* The gleaming brass bell, always polished and always nearby, stood as a silent invitation to end the misery.

But every time I heard its soul-crushing ring as another man gave up, something strange happened. It fueled my resolve.

I noticed a pattern. It wasn't always the average guys like me who were quitting. More often, it was the strongest-looking guys— the ones who looked carved from granite. Watching them break, watching them choose comfort over commitment, only made me dig deeper.

By Hell Week's dawn, only a handful of originals remained in Boat Crew 2. I was leaner, tougher, and finally a true teammate. Phase 1 had tried to break us, but it forged me instead.

I was becoming a monster.

Hell Week arrived under a cold midnight sky, exploding into our lives with shouting, banging trash cans, and fire hose blasts. The week that would define our futures had begun.

Nearly every hour brought new, inventive torture: log PT until our shoulders screamed, boat carries for miles, endless sprints over sand dunes. Sleep became a currency we no longer possessed, doled out in scattered minutes over five and a half grueling days.

My mind began to fray. During one evolution, I hallucinated my mother's pork chops with macaroni and tomato meal so vividly I could taste the grease on my lips. A teammate had to snap me back to reality. Another guy started taking orders from a phantom Abraham Lincoln, saluting empty air with military precision.

Time dissolved into a relentless cycle: cold, pain, exhaustion. The questions echoed in my head on repeat: *What the hell have I gotten myself into? Why am I doing this to myself?*

But our boat crew refused to break. When one man faltered, another shouldered his weight. We crawled through mud thick as concrete. We carried logs that felt like telephone poles. We sang cadences with voices raw as sandpaper, our words disappearing into the wind and waves.

We finished Hell Week with tears of agony and triumph mixing with salt and sand on our faces. Hell Week had nearly broken us, but through grit and brotherhood, we survived.

The monster they were forging was finally taking shape.

After the brute force of Phase 1, we shed our boots for fins and began Phase 2: Dive Phase. The chaos of the grinder gave way to the cold, silent pressure of the deep. Here, trust meant everything. Underwater, you relied on your swim buddy for your very life.

Chief Harlow's words became our scripture: "You don't just swim —you become the water."

We learned to move silently through liquid darkness, to navigate by feel and compass, to become a single, fluid unit in the ocean's vast expanse. In the blackness thirty feet down, your buddy's breathing through the regulator became your heartbeat. His movements became your movements. Survival was partnership.

Three days after finishing Dive Phase, we were back on land for Phase 3: Land Warfare. The scent of chlorine was replaced by gunpowder, oil, and desert dust. This was the final seven-week phase that would prove whether we could operate as the "L" in SEAL.

Weapons training resonated differently than anything before. This was the moment I'd been waiting for since childhood.

As a kid, I'd been obsessed with guns—I had every kind imaginable. Water guns, Nerf guns, dart guns, and my favorite: cap guns. Now, learning to shoot real weapons with purpose and precision, I was transported back to the first real gun I ever encountered.

I was with my best friend Ya-Cob, playing on the front porch of my Aunt Pat's house. Suddenly, he yelled my name with urgency I'd never heard before.

"Jason!"

When I looked over, he was frozen, staring down into a flower pot. I walked over and followed his gaze. There, nestled in black soil like some deadly seed, was a small silver handgun.

Still in play mode, my first instinct was to reach in and grab it. But just before my fingers made contact, something stopped me. This wasn't a toy. This was real.

As mischievous as we were, some deeper instinct took control. We didn't touch it. We knocked on my aunt's door and told her what we'd found. She was raving about how it might be her son, my cousin, Din's gun. She was really mad about, not only, the fact that there's a gun on her property, but how us kids found it and could have hurt ourselves. Later, my grandmother pulled me aside. She told me how proud she was—not just for what I did, but for what *I didn't do.* She knew I had wanted to touch it.

That moment of decision, choosing responsibility over curiosity, was a memory I'd stored away and never revisited. Until now. Standing on a firing range in Coronado, a real weapon in my hands, I finally understood the weight of that childhood choice.

The rest of land warfare blurred together in controlled chaos. On San Clemente Island, we lived with our rifles, survived on scattered sleep, and faced constant surprise attacks. We moved through scrub brush like ghosts, learned to read terrain like scripture, and discovered that exhaustion could be another form of fuel.

By the end, bruised and sand-scarred, we had proved ourselves. We had earned our brown BUD/S shirts and graduated onto SQT.

It took months more of advanced training—learning to jump, shoot, and operate—before the day finally arrived. Chief Harlow moved down the line, pinning a golden Trident on each man's chest.

When he stood before me, I felt the weight of every cold wave, every sand-filled mile, every moment of doubt condensed into that single piece of metal. He pinned it to my chest with ceremony, gave a firm nod of respect, and moved on.

We were no longer candidates. We were brothers.

We were Navy SEALs.

The MONSTER was complete.

The more I thought about that word, the more I remembered my little cousin Kita. When we were kids, she used to call me "Jason the Monster"—not because I was bad, but because of the movie *Friday the 13th*. In her five-year-old mind, the "monster" in the movie shared my name. Jason. She always came up to me giggling, pointin' her finger, and go, 'You Jason the monster!' like it was the funniest thing ever. It was that simple.

Now, I had taken that name to an entirely new level. I gave it new meaning—an acronym born from my journey through hell and transformation.

Military Operations Navy SEAL Trained Elite Recon.

Jason The MONSTER is born.

CHAPTER 6

I'm Back for the First Time

I completed my SEAL training in May 2005. As I earned my Trident, my little brother Kenny was preparing to graduate from high school at Jacob's Center. After training, I was granted a week off for personal and family time, so I caught the next flight back to Cincinnati to see my kid brother walk across that stage.

I left in the same white outfit I'd graduated in, stuffed a few clothes into a bag, and headed straight to the airport.

My mom had given me the details about Kenny's ceremony, but I hadn't promised I'd be there—my arrival was uncertain, so she wasn't expecting me. I wanted it to be a surprise anyway and didn't ask her to pick me up. It wouldn't have mattered; I landed just a couple hours before the ceremony began.

I hailed a cab and told the driver to take me straight to the school. Riding in that backseat, I felt like Larenz Tate in *Dead Presidents*—a soldier coming home to a world that had kept spinning without him.

I slipped into the auditorium just as the ceremony was starting. Instead of searching for my family in the crowd, I hung back, eyes scanning the stage. The first person I spotted was Kenny.

But this wasn't the little brother I remembered.

He was animated, confident, completely out of his shell. He commanded his space on that stage like he owned it. I'd heard he'd spent his senior year playing both basketball and football, and whatever fire those experiences had lit in him was burning brightly now.

From my vantage point, I could see the whole family scattered throughout the auditorium: Aunt Pat and Jalen, Uncle Mike and Aunt Katrina, Uncle Kenny and Aunt Angie, Uncle Steve and Aunt

Vicky. Even Paul Bill, who was married to my late great-grand-mother Nana, was there. Seeing him meant the world—he'd been there for my Navy departure party too.

When the announcer called "Kenneth Jones," Uncle Mike and Uncle Kenny rushed the stage with their cameras like paparazzi. Kenny, beaming with unfiltered swagger, stopped and posed as if he were on a runway, soaking in every second of his moment.

I couldn't have been prouder.

Afterward, as everyone gathered outside for photos, I finally made my move. The wave of shock, then joy, that rippled through my family was electric. My mom's eyes welled up, and she nearly burst into tears. In one day, both her sons were graduates—one from high school, the other from the most grueling military training in the world.

It was, without question, her proudest moment.

Kenny was impeccable in a grey suit and pink vest, his style sharp and uniquely his own. He was bigger too—you could tell he'd been hitting the weights, starting to build a frame like his wrestling hero, Dwayne "The Rock" Johnson, right down to the slick pony-tail. He radiated a presence that was entirely his own.

The celebration naturally continued at Uncle Kenny's house. Walking in, I was hit by memories of my own party there just three years prior. Then, I was a kid with a GED and no clue what was coming. Now, I'd returned as a Navy SEAL, my physique and entire bearing transformed.

My family, who had only seen the change in pictures and heard it in my voice over the phone, was astonished. They peppered me with questions, and I was eager to share the stories.

When I left, only my cousin Din and Caley had children: Din's son, DJ, and Caley's son, Jalen. Since then, Caley and her husband, Gary, had two more children: 3-year-old Jaida and 3-month-old Janiece. This was my first time meeting them.

Catching up with my cousin Mike, we laughed about burying that sock as we discussed Egg McMuffins in the park all those years ago. He asked if I'd seen our childhood friend, Shad, who he said had joined the Navy and shipped out to San Diego in 2003. We had been in the same state, on the same coast, and I never even knew.

The next day, I tagged along with my mom to Aunt Fox's house. As soon as we walked in, Aunt Fox told me how proud she was, then shared something that caught me completely off guard: her husband, Uncle Otis, Big O, as we called him, had served in World War II.

She had never mentioned this before, and I realized she must have felt it necessary to share now because of my own service. I was instantly fascinated. Until then, I'd only seen Uncle Otis in his wheelchair, rarely speaking more than a few words. Now, I felt a connection we'd never shared.

For years, I believed I was the first in my family to wear a uniform besides my mom's late husband, who had also served in the Navy. Yet here was a man I'd known all my life who had played a part in one of the most pivotal wars in American history.

The day before, my family had eagerly listened to my SEAL training stories. Now, it was my turn to sit back and listen to his. He didn't hesitate, opening up and sharing memories I'd never imagined hearing firsthand.
But Big O didn't just tell war stories—he shared the bigger picture.

"We fought two battles," he said, his voice carrying decades of weight. "One for America, and one just to be respected in our own country."

He spoke of segregated units and seeing enemy prisoners receive better treatment than he did. Listening to him, I saw him through completely different eyes—not just as the quiet elder in a wheelchair, but as a man who had carried the weight of history and helped lay the groundwork for future generations, including me.

Our conversation wasn't just an exchange of memories. It was a bond, forged across decades by the shared experience of wearing a uniform and serving with pride.

Later that week, I met up with my brother Nate at his apartment—the same place he'd moved into a couple months before I shipped out for training. Being back brought a wave of memories, reminders of what had changed and what had stayed the same.

Although I'd only met my father's side of the family after turning eighteen, I'd actually met Nate two years earlier when I was sixteen and working at McDonald's. The way we met still felt surreal.

One day at work, as I was dropping fries, a coworker approached with a puzzled look. "Jason, somebody's on the phone for you." I was just as confused—nobody had my work number, not even me. Still, someone was asking for me specifically.

I answered, uncertainty in my voice. "Hello?"

"Hey, what's up, this Jason?"

"Yeah," I replied, more nervous than I wanted to admit, not recognizing the voice.

Then the question that floored me: "Is your dad's name Nate White?"

My heart started pounding. "Yeah?"

"You don't know me, but I'm your brother Nate."

Now, standing in his apartment after SEAL training, that same Nate was grinning ear to ear as he announced he was about to be a father. The thought of having a nephew filled me with excitement. It was hard to believe I'd only known him for a few years. My mind flashed back to the day the phone rang at McDonald's

We all met up at our sister Kisha's place. It felt good to see them again. Donnie, who'd been honorably discharged from the Air Force in 2003—a year after I left for the Navy—was curious about my training and impressed I'd made it through BUD/S.

He reflected on the moment I told him in 2001 that I was trying out for the SEALs. Back then, he didn't think it was a good idea, but now he admitted my decision seemed to be working out. Not so long ago, he was the one the family celebrated when he came home on leave. Now the roles were reversed.

Being around my family during this week off made me realize something important. Yes, joining the military was a way to become a better version of myself, but I was also missing out on the moments that make a family whole.

My little brother had just graduated. My older brother Donnie had settled into civilian life. Nate was about to become a father. All my nieces and little cousins were growing up—right before my eyes and yet also out of reach.

I knew that while I served, I'd likely miss so much: family gatherings, milestones, and the everyday memories that came with being present. The pride I felt in my accomplishments was real, but so was the ache of what I'd have to leave behind.

Spending time at home was a bittersweet reminder that service sometimes means sacrificing not just for the country, but for the people and moments that matter most.

Before heading out again to begin active duty, I made sure to pack the one thing I couldn't bring to boot camp: my camcorder. Before joining the Navy, I carried it everywhere, capturing life as it happened. Now, recording my SEAL journey felt essential.

As I packed, I noticed how my mom saved absolutely everything. She still had my elementary school report cards, and I realized that beyond our usual phone calls, I should start writing letters home. Letter writing is a tradition among people in the military, but for me, the real reason was simple—I knew Mom would treasure those letters, holding onto my words as a diary of my time away.

Whenever I did write, I promised myself to capture every detail, every feeling, so someday she could look back and know exactly where I was on any given day.

On the plane, I watched the world drift by below and reflected on the week I'd spent surrounded by family. I realized how much things had changed and how much I'd already missed. Somehow, being home after so much time away made every moment feel more vivid, more precious.

And as the engines rumbled me back to duty, I couldn't help but think that no matter how many times I return, it's going to always feel like

I'm back for the first time.

CHAPTER 7

I Have Scars I Can't See

June 28, 2005. I was back at the base in Coronado when the word crackled through the compound. A four-man SEAL reconnaissance team was missing in the mountains of Afghanistan—Lt. Michael P. Murphy, Gunner's Mate 2nd Class Danny Dietz, Sonar Technician 2nd Class Matthew Axelson, and Hospital Corpsman 2nd Class Marcus Luttrell.

As a freshly minted SEAL who hadn't even been on my first deployment, their names didn't mean much to me yet. The only thing that mattered was that they were SEALs, lost in the unforgiving mountains of Afghanistan.

A heavy, suffocating silence fell over the barracks. We huddled around radios, the air thick with unspoken prayers. Days bled into one another. Then, the news: Marcus Luttrell had been found, the sole survivor. The rest of his team was gone. In a downed helicopter sent to save them, eight more SEALs and eight Army Night Stalkers had also perished. One of my comrades said it was the worst single loss of life for the SEALs since World War II.

World War II. The words immediately transported me back home, to a quiet man in a wheelchair. Big O.

A few weeks later, I met Marcus Luttrell.

He had just returned, moving through the world with a quietness that was louder than any noise, a slight limp in his gait. Word was he'd rotated out of SEAL Team 10 and was prepping for another deployment to Iraq in 2006. He was eating alone in the chow hall, flipping through a dog-eared copy of *The Art of War.*

I hesitated, then walked over and introduced myself, half expecting to be brushed off.

Instead, he looked up, the exhaustion in his eyes deep enough to drown in. He offered a weary smile. "You're about to learn what brotherhood really means," he said, his voice raspy.

We talked for maybe twenty minutes. He didn't speak of the mission, and I didn't ask. But his eyes told a story of their own—a story of a man who had already seen the end of the world.

Two years later, Marcus Luttrell published a book detailing the events of Operation Red Wings. It was adapted into the movie Lone Survivor in 2013, starring Mark Wahlberg as Marcus.

But that night, all I knew was that I was sitting across from a ghost.

Just a month earlier, I'd been home, a hero in my family's eyes, the newly crowned "Jason The MONSTER." Now, the title felt hollow, almost profane. I was left with a terrifying question: How does anyone survive that kind of hell, and could I?

My own first taste of that hell came just months later, in early 2006, shortly after my nephew Little Nate was born.

We were deployed to Somalia, East Africa.

The sky over Mogadishu never went completely dark. It was more of a murky blue haze—light pollution swirled with dust and tension, broken by the occasional tracer round arcing toward the horizon.

This was the first time in my military career I thought to myself: *What if I never listened to Rivera? What if I never became a Navy SEAL?*

Back home, life was happening without me. What would I be doing right now if I weren't here? Working a welding job, maybe?

Then another thought, just as powerful, washed over me. Wow. I'm really in Africa. My mother's words echoed in my head: *The military can take you places I can't.* And here I was, standing in the motherland, the birthplace of all humanity. But I wasn't here on vacation. I had to quickly snap out of it.

I stepped off the C-130 onto Somali soil with Team 5, boots sinking into heat-baked gravel, eyes scanning shadowy rooftops for movement.

Our mission: anti-piracy operations and hostage recovery.

Midnight, off the coast, our stealth boat cut through the black water toward the hijacked cargo vessel, the MV Brilliance. Sea spray coated my helmet. The wind whispered doubts.

I climbed the hull of the ship in near silence, my heartbeat a frantic drum against my ribs. Movement was spotted. The night exploded in gunfire. I hit the deck, rolling, returning fire, my training taking over my body. We secured the bridge.

One hostage was hit. I carried him down the rope ladder to the medevac boat while my team neutralized the remaining threats. Twenty minutes after we boarded, the mission was over.

And I was forever changed.

Days later, we were on patrol in Mogadishu's Bakara Market. From a distance, it looked festive—brightly colored fabrics, the melodic call to prayer drifting on the air. Up close, it was a hub for arms dealing and human trafficking. I saw a child, no older than eight, clutching a modified AK-47. He wasn't a soldier. He was just a terrified little boy.

And in his face, I didn't see a stranger. I saw my little cousin, Jalen, who was the same age. This place was making my mind play tricks on me. That image is burned into my memory. It will never leave me.

After weeks of missions, our team boarded the USS Bainbridge for decompression. Staring out at the endless, empty ocean, I finally took out a pen and paper to write the first letter home to my mom, just as I'd promised. The first words that came to me were the truest I'd ever written.

"I became a SEAL to be a warrior. Now,

I have scars I can't see."

CHAPTER 8

Move Forward with Love

After our tour in East Africa, my deployment orders changed. In the same year, 2006, I found myself in Iraq.

The heat was the first enemy.

It wrapped around me like a punishment, a physical weight that pressed down on my soul. Ramadi wasn't just hot—it felt cursed. The sun baked the concrete until it shimmered, the air smelled of diesel and despair, and every alley whispered threats through broken satellite dishes.

We landed at Al Asad Airbase, our gear heavy, our minds heavier. Still with SEAL Team 5, we were tasked with locating and capturing high-value insurgent operatives. My training has taught me precision. Iraq taught me unpredictability.

On a night raid, intel had identified a compound where a suspected bomb-maker was operating. Four Humvees rolled quietly through the backstreets, headlights off. My heart thudded against my ribs, a familiar rhythm by now.

"Zulu-5, breach on my mark," the command crackled in my ear.

The world erupted.

Breach. Flashbang. Chaos.

The room was thick with smoke and the metallic tang of cordite. A man darted through the confusion. I gave chase and took him down hard. He was no bomb-maker—just a terrified cook who had been in the wrong place at the wrong time.

Misinformation. We found only traces of the network: burner phones, blueprints, and a photo of a man who would later haunt our next mission.

I quickly learned how intel shifts in seconds. What you prep for isn't always what you find.

I bonded with my team—especially Mac, our breacher, who'd survived two IED blasts and cracked jokes like he had nine lives. I learned to build mental maps: entrances, escapes, the smell of plastic explosives before I even saw them.

After months in the furnace of Africa and Iraq, I was granted a month's leave—stand-down time. After that, I was to report to Washington, D.C.

My first thought was to go home. A month surrounded by family, telling war stories, felt like the perfect antidote to everything I'd seen.

But then I reconsidered. That might not be the best idea.

If I went home now, I might not want to come back.

I really needed to spend this time alone—reflecting, learning the new me, just enjoying life for a moment. So I decided to spend my leave in the Sunshine State: Miami, Florida. A vacation of sorts.

After my leave, we were ordered to Washington D.C. for a debriefing and a visit to the White House. The thought of meeting President Bush brought my brother Donnie's words rushing back: "You don't want to join the military while Bush is in office."

By this time, I'd seen firsthand what kind of president I was dealing with. I'd also seen the Michael Moore documentary *Fahrenheit 9/11*. I'd watched how badly he handled Hurricane Katrina and heard Kanye West say on live television, "George Bush doesn't care about Black people."

I'd come out of SEAL training months before Hurricane Katrina and the breaking of the levees. Some of the people I'd trained with were sent to New Orleans to help out. While my first fight was against men with rifles, theirs was against Mother Nature.

But at the same time, he was the President of the United States. George Bush was in office before I joined the military, and I was warned by my brother. I could have simply not joined. But I did—I made a choice. And with that choice came responsibilities. I had a responsibility to our president, no matter who he was.

So I bottled up any feelings of disdain and shook his hand with respect for the office.

Early in 2007, my phone rang with news from home: my little brother, Kenny, had a son—Kenneth Jones III. I was in shock. Another nephew to look forward to, another reason to hurry back whenever I could. But I couldn't savor it for long; deployment was already looming.

As we geared up for another tour in Iraq, I watched teammates uproot their families every few years, navigate emotional landmines during deployments, and return home to routines that had shifted without them. I saw the guilt, the longing, the compromises. I saw the strained marriages, the children growing up with a parent who was just a voice on a satellite phone.

I respected their sacrifice, but I didn't want it for myself.

During my time in service, I didn't have time to create a family. While others in my unit juggled deployment schedules with phone calls home, I was able to leave without considering the feelings of a spouse or children. I made a conscious decision after witnessing it firsthand: no relationships, no family ties.

I chose solitude.

No one waiting at home meant no hesitation when the orders came.

No emotional negotiations before missions. No fear of leaving someone behind—except my own shadow.

It wasn't loneliness; it was clarity.

Fallujah, 2007. Our team was tasked with extracting an embedded Army intel officer caught during recon. It was supposed to be surgical.

Instead, it was a firefight.

I took cover behind a shattered market stall. Mac was hit—shrapnel to the leg. I dragged him behind the Humvee, returned fire, and covered extraction like I'd done it a thousand times. That was the moment I crossed an invisible line.

I was no longer new.

Later that night, I stared up at the desert sky, still wearing the blood-smeared uniform. I thought of Ohio, of silence, of lives divided by choices. And I realized: Jason The MONSTER was no longer just a name. This was who I was now.

That summer, I met Chris Kyle. He was quiet, calculating, already a legend whispered about in the ranks—"The Devil of Ramadi." We trained together for a week.

CQB drills, sniper overwatch coordination, and urban movement. I wasn't a sniper, but I learned more in those few days than I had in months. Kyle had a way of making you feel like you mattered, even if you were just a new guy.

One night, over a shared MRE, he looked at me and said, "You'll see things you'll never forget. Just make sure you don't lose yourself in them." His words were prophetic.

Like Marcus Luttrell, Chris Kyle later had a movie made about him— American Sniper, where he was played by Bradley Cooper.

While I was engaged in some of the most intense battles overseas, chaos was erupting at home in Cincinnati.

I got a call from my brother Nate. He'd been shot in his apartment. He told me the story, but the thing that hurt him more than the bullet was that our dad had refused to let him recover at his house.

On my way back to the States, my dad's decision to not let Nate take shelter at his house clouded my mind. *What kind of man wouldn't let his son stay with him for a few days after something like that?* I thought.

That single act ignited a dormant rage in me.

Then I remembered my last visit home, hanging out with my dad's side of the family, and all the love they showed me. The love I'd felt from my dad's side of the family on my last visit now felt like a cruel joke. A realization I'd never had before hit me harder than the gunfights I'd just survived.

I thought more and more about how much family time I'd missed growing up. I'd literally missed my entire childhood with my siblings and other family members.

Seeing how much the family loved our grandmother reminded me of how much I'd loved mine on my mother's side. But I didn't really know her. I'd never had the opportunity to love her the way they did, and she'd never known me as I was growing up.

Before I met my dad's side, I'd never really thought about it. It was just "it is what it is." Growing up, I was always aware that my dad was married, and I'd assumed my siblings already knew about me. But when I met them, it turned out they'd never even known I existed.

That hurt.

So not only was I kept away from them—I was also a secret. And getting to know them, I started asking myself: *Why? Why was I kept away from my own family growing up?*

There was only one person who could answer that question.

My dad.

As soon as I landed, with ill feelings in my heart, I called him and confronted him about everything: about keeping me a secret, about the lost years, about abandoning Nate in his time of need.

Emotions came out of me that I didn't even know existed. We were both surprised.

I'd never talked to him like this before, and my conversation with him was so loud that some of my comrades came to check on me, assuming I was arguing with some woman, not knowing I was talking to my dad this way.

I expected him to push back, to make excuses. Instead, he just listened. And when I was done, he apologized. He explained his past without making excuses and admitted he was wrong.

"I regret what happened," he said, his voice heavy with the weight of years. "But we still have a whole future ahead of us. I'm willing to make it right."

With that, my emotions shifted. I forgave him.

The conversation shifted to the East Africa and Iraq tours I had just come off of, and he went on to say that he'd served in the Marine Corps in 1972. This was something I'd never known. After high school, he'd joined after his brother—my Uncle Hershel—enlisted.

We spoke on the phone for maybe another hour and decided to put the past behind us and

move forward with love.

CHAPTER 9

Shoot First, Then Aim

The military had consumed my life—it wasn't just what I did; it was who I'd become. I wasn't focused solely on the Navy SEALs anymore. After meeting the president, my fascination deepened into something closer to obsession.

Even in my downtime, the military stayed with me. Vacations weren't for relaxing—they were for studying. I buried myself in history books, military documentaries, and war films I'd ignored before—Platoon, A Few Good Men—and rewatched favorites through new eyes. Military eyes. I didn't just want to serve anymore. I wanted to understand everything about the life I'd chosen.

Learning languages became part of that obsession. I started with Spanish, mostly because I'd been introduced to it in elementary school. Using Rosetta Stone, I taught myself to read, write, and speak it well enough to get by. Then I set a goal to travel where it was spoken—Cancún, Mexico was first.

From there, I moved on to Arabic, hoping to understand the languages I heard in Afghanistan and Iraq. That one didn't last long —it drained me, and I couldn't see using it after the military. French came next, inspired by a planned trip to Paris. I learned just enough to say I spoke "a little French," and that was good enough for me.

Travel soon became part of my identity. Whether for work or on my own dime, hopping a flight felt as routine as someone else driving to the store. A line from a movie, a scene in a documentary, a single mention in a book—any of it could send me halfway across the world.

When people debated flat Earth theories online, saying that seeing the 24-hour sun in Antarctica should end the argument, I took it as a challenge. I didn't believe the Earth was flat, but the idea of seeing a sun that never set fascinated me. The thought alone had me booking a flight before I even realized how rare of a trip that was.

Even though I was trained in hand-to-hand combat as a SEAL, I wanted more. Martial arts had been part of my childhood—my heroes were the Ninja Turtles and the Power Rangers. My brother Kenny was usually my practice dummy, while Ya-Cob and I made our own nunchucks and swatted lightning bugs under the street-lights. Joining a martial arts gym as an adult felt like circling back to those roots.

Mentally, I stayed sharp. Physically, I coasted. I worked out only when I needed to, not making it a habit. That changed when I was deployed alongside David Goggins.

When we met, I was sitting around waiting for orders. He walked up, asked who I was, and one of the guys said, "That's Jason—THE MONSTER."

"Monster?" Goggins smirked. "Then why's he sitting around getting soft?"

From that moment, my life picked up a different pace. Goggins didn't stop. Ever. He didn't believe in excuses or downtime. You couldn't even complain around him without feeling ridiculous. When I told him about my mom whooping me at eight, he laughed and said he got "beat by the Devil himself." I didn't get it at the time—but years later, after reading his book Can't Hurt Me, I understood.

Because of him, I built a daily routine that stuck with me for years. Up at 0500. A hundred push-ups before the day even started. Light breakfast, then two hours at the gym—most hotels had one, and if I could find a 24-hour spot, even better. The rest of my time went to studying, working on languages, or writing raps like I used to back at Job Corps.

By 2009, something felt different. I'd written over thirty letters to my mom, sent photos and videos burned to DVD so my family could see my world. I hadn't been home since Kenny graduated high school in 2005. Instead of returning after deployments, I traveled, filling the space between wars with new landscapes and stories.

But that year, the country shifted. A new president—Barack Obama. Seeing the first Black president sworn in at his inauguration felt like history itself shaking my hand. I didn't get to meet him that day, but a few months later, before another Iraq tour, I did.

Meeting President Bush had been nerve-wracking, formal. Meeting Obama felt entirely different—energizing, personal. I could breathe around him.

Not long after, during some downtime in Texas, I met a man named Orlando at a bar over a game of pool. He was older, ex-Army, and had once tried out for the SEALs. We traded stories, and somewhere between shots on the table, he hit me with a question I hadn't prepared for.

"So… what's your plan?"

It struck me. I didn't have one. Becoming a SEAL had always been the plan. I'd achieved that—so what now?

He pressed further. "You plan to retire from the military? Got an exit plan?"

I didn't. Never thought about it. He told me he wished he'd used the military to set himself up after service—gone to school, learned something new. His words stuck with me like a seed taking root.

Soon after, I enrolled in college. I started business classes and added Audio Video Production on top. I figured, if my future was uncertain, I might as well understand both business and the camera I loved.

That same year, my mom turned fifty. She wanted a big celebration, and my aunt—her older sister Pat—helped plan it. I wired $2,000 from overseas to help make it happen, promising to come if my schedule allowed—but only if it'd be a surprise.

My deployment ended early that January. Suddenly, I could make it home for her birthday in February.

Five years had passed since I'd last set foot in Cincinnati. I flew home the day before the party, met up with my dad and my brothers—Nate and Donnie—and we did what we'd always done: rode around, visited family, and caught up on years in a single afternoon. I got to meet my nephew, Little Nate, for the first time. Also, my dad introduced me to Razz, the new woman in his life.

The next day, with my uniform pressed and a bouquet of red roses in hand, I walked into my mom's birthday party unannounced. Aunt Pat called out, "Debra, you have a visitor," and when Mom turned around, she nearly fainted. She held me tight for what felt like forever, crying and laughing all at once.

The room was packed with family, old and new. My cousin Din was there with his wife Toni and their son Caleb. Din's other son, Mark, couldn't make it, but his name still came up in conversation like he'd just stepped outside. My cousin Caley's son Jalen was eleven now, taller and older than the boy I remembered. Her daughters, Jaida and Janiece, were no longer babies—they were talking, moving, and staring at me like I'd walked out of one of the stories they'd heard their whole lives.

Janiece—everybody called her NeNe—had just turned four on the eleventh. She marched right up to me like we'd known each other for years.

"So, you're my cousin? They say you're a SEAL. Why would you want to be a seal? Why not a shark? A shark is more vicious."

I burst out laughing and explained what SEAL stood for, but I had to admit, in her world, that logic checked out.

I met my Uncle Mike's soon-to-be wife, Denise, and her son Luke. Him and Katrina were no longer together. Uncle Mike's son—my cousin Jay—had just married a young woman named Brittney a few months earlier in 2009. My Aunt Debbie introduced me to her husband Ron, and seeing her happy with him added another layer of joy to the night. My cousin Tionne now had a ten-month-old daughter named Skylar with a woman named Qyanna, and holding that little girl felt like holding time itself.

But the moment that hit closest to home was meeting my other new nephew, Little Kenny. Looking at him, knowing everything his dad and I had been through growing up, made the night feel even bigger than just a birthday party.

Me and my cousin Mike still laughed about burying that sock in the park all those years ago. He asked if I'd seen his childhood friend Shad, and I realized I'd forgotten he'd joined the Navy right after me.

The whole night was filled with love, surprises, and a nonstop circle of people asking for stories from "over there." I gave them what I could without bringing the war into the room.

On that trip, I also found out my mom no longer lived in the house on Larona—the house I grew up in. It hit harder than I expected. There were so many memories in that place, and now I couldn't just walk through the door anymore. The next day, I drove over anyway and sat outside, just looking at it.

While I was in the neighborhood, I checked the old block on Burnet Ave, parking by J&W, the corner store I'd walked to a thousand times as a kid. Faces I hadn't seen in years were still there, holding down the same stretch of sidewalk. Then I drove down Rockdale and saw that my elementary school had been torn down and rebuilt. The building where I'd learned to read, write, and met my best friend Ya-Cob no longer existed. That hit almost as hard as the house on Larona.

I drove up Northern Ave and passed Nita and Sam's place—my old babysitters' house, my second home growing up. The streets were the same, but everything felt different.

That visit home made me realize more than I expected. For the first time, I felt something I didn't like admitting: I didn't want to go back. But I still had a duty. And now, I had a new mission.

Last time I left home, I made sure to pack my camcorder for the road. This time, I came back determined to take the past with me. I gathered all my old home videos—from the tapes I'd shot growing up to the ones I'd dubbed from my Uncle Kenny years earlier: Christmas '93 and '94, the family picnic from '92, all of it. Now that I was taking Audio Video classes, I knew I could finally do something with those old recordings—clean them up, stitch them together, and turn them into something my family could hold onto forever.

On the flight back to base, I thought about Orlando at that pool table in Texas and his questions about my future. His words echoed again: *What's your plan?* Joining the military had been the best decision I could have made at the time. It gave me drive, discipline, and skills I never would've had otherwise. But how long could I really keep doing this without getting hurt or killed? I'd attended enough funerals to know that nobody beat the odds forever.

In the military, we're trained to aim first, then shoot. In life, I'd done the opposite.

When I decided to become a Navy SEAL, that was me shooting first—taking a wild, life-changing shot with no clear plan for what came after. I hadn't thought about college, retirement, or what life would look like beyond the teams.

My contract ended in 2015, and at first, my only options in my head were to reenlist or get out completely with an honorable discharge. But now I saw another path: going into the Navy SEAL Reserves. That way, I could stay in, reach retirement in seven more years—2022—and at the same time start merging back into civilian life.

That became the plan. And I knew I probably never would've come up with it without that conversation with Orlando planting the seed.

Joining was the shot. Everything that came after—that was the aim.

Sometimes, you have to

shoot first, then aim.

CHAPTER 10

The Face of the First Death

The universe has a strange way of reminding you of the cycle of life and death, even when you think you've become numb to it. Just a few months after my mother's 50th birthday celebration in 2010, the somber call came in June of 2012. Another death, another funeral I had to attend, another essential pause in the rhythm of my life.

Uncle Otis.

The man we called, "Big O." He was mostly quiet and primarily stayed home, the old man who always seemed to be observing from his wheelchair, his mind perhaps a thousand miles and decades away. I had shared one of those rare, profound moments with him not long ago, a quiet exchange where he opened up about his service in World War II. That shared memory, a silent nod to a brotherhood of service across generations, made this news hit differently.

My family's history with service and loss stretched back decades. I remember my mother's late husband, Kenny, who died tragically young in 1986 when my brother was a mere two months old. He had served in the Navy, a detail I carried with me. Five years later, in 1991, Kenny's mother—our beloved Grandma Fanny—passed away.

Grandma Fanny's funeral was etched in my mind for a specific, powerful reason. During the viewing, a man—a complete stranger to me, yet clearly bound to her by some deep tie—stood weeping openly at the casket. He was dressed in a crisp, Army-green service uniform. His grief was palpable, a raw, unrestrained sorrow that commanded the room's attention.

Then, in a moment of quiet ceremony that transcended the formality of the service, he took off his military hat and placed it gently in the casket with her. It was a gesture of final respect, a silent farewell from one part of her life to the next.

That moment, that deeply personal and solemn act of placing the service cap, crystallized an unspoken tradition for me. I vowed that I would adopt that sacred action at any of my family's funerals where they were being laid to rest.

Now, standing on the precipice of Big O's final service, I realized he would be the first.

The funeral home was hushed, filled with the low murmur of familial grief and whispered condolences. It was the viewing portion, the quiet hour before the official service began. I could hear the soft drone of my family's hushed conversations as I walked through the door.

I was dressed in my stark white service uniform, a deliberate choice that made me stand out against the sea of black and gray.

As I entered the room, the conversations faltered and died away. A sudden silence fell over the place, all eyes turning toward the uniform. I ignored the attention, my focus fixed on one destination: Big O's casket.

I walked directly to it and stood at attention. In that moment, the entire room seemed to hold its breath. I stood in silence, absorbing the reality of his absence, then slowly, ceremoniously, I removed my white military hat and held it pressed against my chest.

A realization swept over me: this was not just my moment; it was a tribute to a lineage of service and the family matriarch who had inspired the gesture. I turned and walked purposefully toward the front row, where Aunt Fox, Big O's devoted wife of many years, sat. Her face was etched with a sorrow that went bone-deep.

I knelt down beside her, the stiff material of my uniform creasing slightly. I gently took her hand, a small comfort in the face of immense loss. "Aunt Fox," I asked, my voice low and respectful, "I'd like to place my service hat in Big O's casket as a final salute. Would you do me the honor of accompanying me?"

She nodded slowly, a single tear tracking down her cheek, but her eyes held a spark of pride and appreciation. I helped her up, and together—the uniformed descendant and the grieving widow—we walked back to Big O's final resting place.

I didn't want to simply perform the act; I wanted her to be the one to complete it. I handed my crisp white hat to Aunt Fox. "Please," I murmured, "do the honors."

With a trembling hand, she took the cap—a symbol of my own life's commitment—and placed it gently in the casket. She positioned it right below where his hands rested peacefully, a silent white anchor against the dark velvet lining.

It was a shared farewell, a tradition honored, and a final, enduring salute from one generation of service to another.

Reverend Rousseau O'Neal II, the pastor of Rockdale Baptist, delivered the eulogy.

When the service was over, the family went to the cemetery for the burial. As the bugle played "Taps," I stood at attention, rendering a final salute to a fellow serviceman, a family member, and a hero. The 21-gun salute echoed across the quiet field, the sharp cracks a final, harsh punctuation mark on a life well-served.

I watched as the flag was carefully folded into a perfect triangle, a symbol of a grateful nation. An officer approached Aunt Fox, knelt, and presented the flag to her.

The family gathered at Uncle Kenny's place—the house that had always been the center of our celebrations—for the repast. To my surprise, it wasn't the same house anymore. They'd moved out of the big place where I'd once celebrated earning my GED and my going-away party before leaving for the Navy. We shared food and stories in this new space, carrying old memories into new walls.

My cousin Tionne personally invited me to his upcoming wedding this September. He's marrying Qyanna, whom I met at my mom's 50th birthday party. It's hard to believe their daughter, Skylar, is already two; she was only ten months old when I first met her!

I jokingly told him, 'If I'm not overseas shooting bad guys, I'll be there.

On top of that, my brother Kenny had a new girlfriend he'd met just two months prior. He was eager to introduce us.

'This is my girlfriend, Jen,' he said, then turned to her with a grin. 'Jen, this is my brother Jason—the Navy SEAL.'

You could hear the excitement in his voice when he said it, but I couldn't resist. I jokingly corrected him, 'It's *Jason The Monster*.'

Kenny cracked up immediately, and Jen joined right in, laughing along with us.

Big O wasn't the first family member I lost while I was committed to my service. In 2007, years before, my Great-Grandmother Nana's husband, Paul Bill, passed away. His death was a significant loss, but the demands of my deployment made it impossible for me to return home for his service. I had to mourn from a distance, a common, painful reality for those of us in the military.

Then, late in 2011, I received news that Daniel Hughes had passed away. Dan had been a significant figure in our past—the man my mother had dated, and the reason we had embarked on a memorable trip to Detroit back in 1996.

Dan was more than just my mother's temporary partner; he was an active father figure to Kenny and me. For a while, he even moved into our house, creating a blended, bustling household. That summer in '96 was particularly memorable, as his children came down from Detroit to stay with us.

Some of us ended up attending Woodward High School together. Though Dan and my mother never married, a brotherhood had already been forged. His kids became my "brothers and sisters from Detroit," a simple, shared label of our unique kinship.

Hearing about Dan's death brought a wave of sadness. I learned that he had moved to California before his passing. While I couldn't make it to his funeral, I genuinely wished I could have been there to say goodbye and to support the family we had all become a part of. His memory remained a powerful reminder of that transformative period in my life, and the enduring nature of bonds formed outside the traditional family structure.

Big O's funeral, however, marked a different kind of milestone. It was the first family funeral I had been able to attend since I joined the military—a grim reunion with the civilian world.

But while I missed those family goodbyes, I was no stranger to the rituals of loss. My time in uniform had already brought me to countless gravesides, standing in stark, silent formation for my fallen comrades.

I came into the military, especially an elite special operations force like the SEAL Team, with full awareness that death was a fundamental part of the job. It was a subject we trained for, planned for, and executed. The focus of that awareness, though, was always external. I thought about the death we would bring—the calculated, necessary violence directed at the enemy. My mind was consumed with mission success and the casualties we were meant to inflict.

What I hadn't fully prepared myself for, what the training manuals didn't quite capture, was the stark reality of loss on our side. I was naive to believe that our elite status or rigorous training offered a shield from the ultimate price.

The funerals of my teammates—men I had trusted with my life, men who had become closer than family—were a brutal, recurrent lesson in the mortality we all shared. Each one was a visceral reminder that the dangers we faced were not just tactical problems, but deeply personal ones.

The death I brought was a weapon. The death that found us was a wound.

One of the most heartbreaking and unforgettable funerals I have ever attended was for Jon Tumilson, known as JT, a SEAL who was killed in action. The sorrow was palpable, a heavy blanket over the gathering, but what made the experience truly unique and soul-crushing was the presence of his loyal companion.

His dog.

The Labrador, Hawkeye, was not just an attendee; he was a mourner. Throughout the service, as speakers offered eulogies and family members wept, Hawkeye remained steadfastly by the flag-draped casket. He didn't roam or whine; he simply laid on the floor, his massive head resting near the foot of the coffin.

It was an undeniable, gut-wrenching moment where the concept of a "dumb animal" was obliterated. The dog's stillness, his quiet vigilance, spoke volumes. It was as if he understood the finality of the ceremony, the gravity of the occasion. He seemed to know, with heartbreaking certainty, that the person inside that polished box was his master, the man who had shared his life, his home, and his love.

That silent vigil of a faithful dog, refusing to leave the side of his fallen hero, cemented the event in my memory as a raw, powerful testament to unconditional loyalty and loss.

But by far, the largest and most moving funeral I have ever attended was for Chris Kyle, famously known as The American Sniper. It was a somber yet deeply respectful farewell for a true American hero.

I had the distinct honor and privilege of having trained alongside Chris years prior, an experience that left an indelible mark on me, showcasing his professionalism, skill, and genuine character. He was, and remains, a colossal figure in the history of the U.S. Navy SEAL teams, credited with 160 confirmed kills during his tours, making him the most lethal sniper in American military history.

When his memoir, *American Sniper: The Autobiography of the Most Lethal Sniper in U.S. Military History was* published the year before his tragic death, I was one of the very first people to secure a copy. I devoured it, recognizing the authenticity and raw honesty of the experiences he detailed—experiences that I had glimpsed first-hand during our time training together.

His book was more than just a recounting of military service; it was a window into the mind and heart of a warrior who carried an immense burden of responsibility, and who ultimately sought to serve his country and his fellow service members.

The scale of the funeral was a testament to the immense respect and gratitude the nation held for him, a heartbreaking yet fitting tribute to a man who lived and died by the SEAL ethos.

The act of taking a human life, even one necessitated by the grim realities of war, did not come naturally to me. Despite the relentless, high-intensity training engineered to strip away any hesitation and condition us for lethal efficiency, the internal cost was profound.

There is a fundamental violation in ending another person's existence, a seismic shift deep within the psyche that, if left unchecked, becomes a slow, corrosive poison. It is this gnawing internal change, this potential for self-destruction, that drives my relentless pursuit of activity. I keep myself constantly engaged, always in motion, a deliberate, frantic effort to outrun the shadow of guilt I know is always trailing me.

I have witnessed the devastating toll of Post-Traumatic Stress Disorder on my brothers-in-arms, and I wage a constant, personal war to avoid that same fate.

My primary defense against this guilt is a rigid, internal narrative: I tell myself that every life I took was a sacrifice made for the sake of this nation. My hands are stained, but only in service to the United States. I have a clean conscience regarding the innocent; I have never spilled their blood. My targets were always those identified as the enemy, individuals I was tasked to neutralize.

The calculus was brutally simple and existential: if I hesitated, if I failed to pull the trigger, they would most certainly have killed me and my teammates. This conviction is the anchor that prevents me from drifting into the abyss of self-condemnation.

My first confirmed kill occurred amidst the scorched earth and chaos of Iraq. Prior to that moment, I had fired hundreds of rounds at insurgent positions—a blur of kinetic energy and noise—but had no verifiable hits, no certainty that my bullets had found a mark.

The first time I knew I had taken a life unfolded in the breathless intensity of one of our countless engagements. In the heat of that firefight, an Iranian operative somehow managed to close the distance, darting across the open ground and heading straight for my position. He came close enough for me to distinctly register the sharp, angular features of his face, the intensity in his eyes.

I was concealed behind a massive, sun-baked boulder, an advantage he failed to perceive. It was a lapse in situational awareness that cost him everything, and for me, it was a crucial gift of time. He was running with his weapon shouldered, not ready to engage, while my rifle was already up, sighted, and prepared to deliver a verdict.

I exploded from cover, my finger already indexed on the trigger. With a smooth, calculated pull—a single, sharp discharge—a person's life was extinguished.

In that fraction of a second, as the battle raged in fast-forward around me, that specific moment of execution seemed to plunge into slow motion. I got a stark, indelible look at his face—the moment of shock, the sudden, terrible realization, and then the absence.

It was a face branded into my memory, a ghost I could never banish.

And here lies the most disturbing psychological reality of my career: that first face became the only face.

Every subsequent kill carried the weight of that original encounter.

As I accrued more kills, the act itself became mechanically easier. The professional detachment hardened into a practiced reflex. But the strangest, most unnerving phenomenon was the consistency of the faces.

No matter who my target was—tall or short, dark-skinned or

light, male or female—they were all unique individuals in the split-second before I pulled the trigger. Yet the instant their life force was gone, a horrifying transformation occurred. Their features would suddenly morph, superimposed or replaced entirely by the memory of the first man I killed.

It was an eerie, dissociative experience, like the glitching of a virtual world. It felt as if I wasn't killing a succession of unique enemies, but rather a single, looping character in a grim video game. I just kept killing the same man, over and over, in different uniforms and different locales.

Across my ten years of service as a Navy SEAL—a decade defined by deployments, precision, and violence—I have a confirmed kill count of seventy-six.

And when the final life I was responsible for taking ended, I did not see a stranger.

I still only saw

the face of the first death.

CHAPTER 11

A SEAL's Farewell

With my business and audio-video coursework finally completed, I immediately enrolled in real estate classes. I saw this as a viable career path I could pursue once my active duty concluded. My rationale was simple: as long as I was serving, I needed to constantly be in some form of schooling or training, primarily because the military was covering the tuition entirely. This was a crucial opportunity to amass as many valuable skills and credentials as possible—a deliberate strategy to build a robust professional foundation completely outside the operational context of the battlefield.

When I wasn't engrossed in my studies or fulfilling my military duties, I would often spend my downtime editing and refining the home videos I had brought back to base. This served as a creative outlet and a way to maintain the audio-video skills I had acquired. The combination of military discipline, academic pursuit, and creative technical work became the defining rhythm of my life during those years.

The year was 2014, and my training in Audio Video Production was about to intersect with my life as a Navy SEAL in a completely unexpected way.

One day, I was called into my superior's office. He was a man of few words, and his expression was usually unreadable. I braced myself. In my line of work, a summons from a superior often meant a deployment, an intense new training evolution, or perhaps a sudden mission.

But what he told me caught me completely off guard. He leaned forward slightly, a hint of a smile playing on his lips.

"Hey, you were taking Audio Video classes, right?" he asked, his tone casual.

"Yes, sir," I replied instantly, already wondering where this was going.

He paused, letting the silence hang in the air, then delivered the second question.

"And you trained with Chris Kyle, correct?"

The name hit me. Chris. The legendary American Sniper. I went silent for a moment, the memories flooding back. "Yes, sir, I did," I confirmed.

He nodded. "They're making a movie about his book, *American Sniper*," he announced. "Kevin Lacz is already signed on as a technical advisor. They want some other SEALs involved too, for background, extras, general guidance."

He paused, then added with a wry smirk, "This can give you a well-deserved break from getting shot at by enemies. Instead, you can get shot at by Clint Eastwood with his camera crew. He's directing this thing, after all." He let the absurdity of the comparison sink in. "So, are you in?"

The decision was instantaneous. It wasn't just a break; it was a chance to honor Chris and contribute to the accurate portrayal of our brotherhood. "Yes sir, count me in," I responded.

And just like that, because my superior officer remembered I held an Audio Video degree and had trained with Chris Kyle, I was offered an incredible opportunity: to help bring the true story of a SEAL icon to the silver screen.

I didn't do much on set besides offer some input and work as an extra. Even then, you wouldn't know it was me—I was hidden behind headgear the whole time. Mostly, I walked around with my camcorder, documenting the experience for myself. But I wasn't shy about claiming my fame. Whenever I watched the movie with someone, I made sure to point myself out. I remember telling my brother Nate, "Imma be larger than that nigga Steven Seagal, Imma be a big-ass movie star," quoting O-Dog from *Menace II Society*. We burst out laughing. That was our dynamic—communicating through a constant stream of movie quotes.

As 2015 approached, my time on active duty was winding down. I was transitioning to the Navy SEAL Reserves and knew I wanted to be back in Cincinnati. Since I still had drill one weekend a month and two weeks a year, I kept my small place in California, but I needed a home base in Ohio. The long-term plan was to build my dream home eventually, so I started looking for a temporary spot—something modest that would be easy to resell.

While scrolling through Zillow, one listing stopped me cold. It gave me chills, but it also sparked a fantastic idea. *This is perfect,* I thought. Instead of buying a bachelor pad just to sell it later, I could buy this place for my mom. Her 55th birthday was coming up, and this way, the house would stay in the family forever.

Because I now had my realtor license, the house wasn't hard for me to secure.

I bought the house, furnished it, and invited the whole family over for a "birthday party." I set everything up so that would be the moment she saw it for the first time. When the day came, I had my brother Kenny drive Mom to her soon-to-be new home while she was blindfolded. The rest of the family was already in the driveway, waiting.

They pulled in, and I helped her out of the car, guiding her to stand in the front yard. When Kenny pulled off the blindfold, she wasn't just looking at a house. She was standing in front of 118 Woolper Ave.

My grandparents' house. Her parents' house.

It was the same home where my grandmother lived until she passed in '94, and my grandfather until '95. Aunt Pat had lived there for a few years after that, and then Uncle Mike, who renovated it before selling it out of the family. But now, the circle was closed. My mom could finally call her mother's house "home" again.

Upon transitioning into my role as a Navy Reservist, I was confronted with the immediate need to maintain a productive schedule. Despite the security of my existing military pay, the desire for continued professional engagement, coupled with my realtor license, propelled me to seek civilian employment. However, a traditional 9-to-5 workday was a non-starter. Having dedicated thirteen years of my life to the military, I was determined to avoid the constraints of a conventional office job. My next venture had to offer autonomy, flexibility, and control over my own time, which made real estate the perfect fit.

Beyond the immediate professional opportunities, my military career had forged a powerful network. The sheer volume of people I had met, particularly during my extended time in California and my brief experience on a movie set, laid the groundwork for finding remote, flexible work.

It was around this time that I made a connection that would redefine my post-active-duty life: Steve Lobel. The encounter occurred in California, after a long day of filming for *American Sniper*. I was out with a few friends at a nightclub when I first noticed him. Initially, I didn't recognize the music industry veteran, but his choice of attire—a Bone Thugs-n-Harmony t-shirt—was the immediate catalyst for our interaction.

"Hey man, I love that shirt, I gotta get me one," I said, approaching him. "That's my favorite rap group."

He smiled and responded, "Mine too, that's why I manage them."

His declaration was delivered with such casual confidence that I assumed he was joking. I decided to play along.

"That's what's up," I countered. "I'm a Navy SEAL. They need a bodyguard for their upcoming E. 1999 Eternal tour? I can be their personal tour guard."

The idea, delivered as a jest, immediately captured his attention. "That's actually not a bad idea," he mused. "You're an active SEAL now?"

"Yup, until next year," I confirmed, then continued the playful exaggeration: "I'm a movie star too, I'm working on a movie called *American Sniper*," deliberately overstating my minor role.

We continued the conversation, and at one point, Steve pulled out his phone. He began listing the cities where Bone Thugs-n-Harmony would be touring, clearly detailing the logistics. It was in that moment I realized I had misjudged the situation—he genuinely was their manager.

We exchanged contact information, and just a few months later, in March of 2015, Steve called. The conversation was brief and direct. Before I knew it, I was officially hired and preparing to hit the road with Bone Thugs-n-Harmony as a personal bodyguard for the tour.

The tour's early stops brought the group close to home, beginning in the Midwest with shows in Indiana, followed by Cleveland and, most excitingly, Cincinnati. For the Cincinnati show, I made sure to use my unique access to share the experience with those closest to me. My brother Kenny and his girlfriend Jen were there, along with my best friend Ya-Cob.

Looking back on my life, which included intense military training, global deployments, and the inherent dangers of being a Navy SEAL, the feeling of standing on stage with Bone Thugs-n-Harmony was an unparalleled experience. It was a moment of pure, unexpected civilian triumph that transcended the high-stakes world I had just left behind.

By this time, Facebook had become a massive phenomenon. I had always known about it, but given my line of work and growing up in the 90s, voluntarily broadcasting my every move wasn't something I was eager to do. But my family and friends wouldn't stop talking about it. They insisted it was the best way to keep up with the family and that I'd be surprised by how many old friends I could reconnect with. That convinced me.

I created an account and started with the basics—close family first, then schoolmates from Aiken, Woodward, and all the way back to Rockdale Elementary. Then, I remembered one person I absolutely needed to find. I hadn't seen him since we were teenagers, right before I joined Job Corps. Before that, our last real time together was at Grandma Fanny's funeral. Not my brother Kenny, but Kenny's biological brother from his dad's side, my stepbrother. It was Jayson

Jayson and I were close as kids, bonded by our age and the fact that we shared a name, even if he spelled his with a 'Y.' But after his dad died in '86 and Grandma Fanny in '91, he went back to Philadelphia, and we drifted apart. I figured he'd be easy to find with two key factors: the 'Y' in his name and the city of Philadelphia. I was right. I found him, sent a friend request, and shot him a direct message explaining who I was. A few days later, he responded. Just like that, Kenny and I were finally reconnected with our Philadelphia brother after all those years.

As the long days of 2015 began to give way to autumn, a much-anticipated event was brewing: a Family Reunion organized by my dad's side of the family. The prospect filled me with profound excitement. This wasn't just another casual gathering; it was set to be the first significant, large-scale assembly with this part of my heritage since that watershed moment fourteen years earlier, in 2001, when I first met them.

The memory of that initial meeting remains as vivid as if it happened yesterday. At that time in my life, it was, without a doubt, the single most anticipated and pivotal moment I had ever experienced.

For my entire childhood, I lived with the distinct knowledge that I had siblings—brothers and sisters—on my father's side, whom I had never met. I always harbored the assumption that they, too, were aware of my existence. However, the reality of that first encounter, particularly when I met my brother Nate, revealed the surprising truth: that assumption was completely unfounded. The majority of my family on my dad's side had no idea I was even alive.

The moment I finally stood face-to-face with them delivered the most incredible, soul-satisfying feeling in the world. It was as if a crucial, long-missing piece of my personal puzzle had finally clicked into place.

The news that there was a new member of the family—me—spread quickly. The very first person I met was my sister Keisha, accompanied by her adorable three-year-old daughter, Ki'Aisa. While I had the comfort of a brother growing up, this moment forged a completely new type of relationship. I now had a sister, and even more wonderfully, I had a niece. I was, for the first time, an uncle.

Following that initial breakthrough, the introductions continued, and I met the rest of my newfound family.

The setting of that monumental night was in June, a vibrant, warm evening. Nate was the first to arrive at my house. Close behind him was my brother Donnie, who had just completed the long drive up from Texas, pulling up alongside our cousin Nick. The destination for the evening was a party being held at my Uncle Jr.'s house—my dad's brother.

That night was a whirlwind of introductions and connections. Meeting all my cousins, aunts, and uncles for the first time immersed me in a state of pure euphoria, a joy so intense and overwhelming that, to this day, it has never been truly matched.

That is, until the family reunion in 2015.

This reunion felt like meeting everyone all over again, but with deeper context. During my time in active military service, my visits home were sporadic, and while I always made an effort to spend time with some of the family, I rarely had the chance to see them all together in one place.

Upon arriving at the reunion and working the room, my cousin Rally introduced me to his wife, Christina. It was Christina who, in turn, introduced me to her cousin, Torri.

As I was meeting Torri, I was struck by an inexplicable sense of familiarity. It wasn't a recent memory, but a vague, distant recognition—someone I felt I had glimpsed in the background of my life when I was much younger.

"You look so familiar," I confessed to her, trying to place her face. "What school did you go to?"

"I went to Woodward," she replied simply.

"Woodward, yes, that sounds exactly right," I mused. Driven by the need to resolve the puzzle, I pressed further. "I feel like I didn't know you directly, but I definitely knew someone you used to spend time with."

Torri began to rattle off a list of names, and as she spoke, one name leaped out and instantly anchored the memory: Dorothy.

"Dorothy! That's exactly who I remember seeing you with! Dorothy Hyneman, right?"

A genuine smile lit up her face. "Yes, that's my sister."

"For real? Your sister? That's what's up!" I exclaimed. "I went to elementary school with her."

We then settled into the comfortable pattern of catching up, exchanging the essential questions: How have you been? What have you been up to since those high school days? It was a small-world moment that made the massive reunion feel intensely personal.

The success and joy of that 2015 reunion set a wonderful precedent. Over the subsequent two years, we continued the tradition, holding two more successful family reunions in 2016 and 2017, solidifying the bonds that were once so tenuous and making up for all the lost time.

The curtain had closed on the era of the Obama Administration, marking a significant shift in the nation's political landscape with the inauguration of a new president: Donald J. Trump. My first encounter with him came after my time on active duty had concluded. Yet the sensation I felt in his presence was a surprising blend of my previous experiences meeting both George W. Bush and Barack Obama.

There was the familiar gravity that accompanies meeting the Commander-in-Chief—a feeling of respect for the office, much like the atmosphere that surrounded my meeting with President Bush. But simultaneously, there was an unmistakable energy, a sense of rapid change and dynamic personality that echoed the powerful drive I had sensed during my time with President Obama.

This unexpected synthesis of feelings made the meeting with President Trump a uniquely memorable experience. It wasn't merely meeting a new leader; it was witnessing a new, unpredictable chapter of American history unfold in person.

Towards the close of 2018, a profound sadness settled over my family as my Aunt Fox reached the final stage of her battle with cancer. She was residing in a nursing home, a place of waiting, where the relentless disease was poised to finally claim her. The inevitable day arrived in February of 2019.

Aunt Fox, a woman of deep faith and quiet strength, passed away. In her passing, she found the peace she had been so courageously seeking.

The arrangements were made, and her funeral was held at Rockdale Baptist Church. As I prepared for the service, a solemn promise I had made to myself years earlier resurfaced with clarity. It was a vow made during the funeral of Big O. I had promised myself that when Aunt Fox's day came, I would attend the service in my full military uniform and bring my service hat to place inside her casket—a final salute to a life well-lived and deeply loved.

That initial action was tragically followed by another profound loss just a few months later, in October of that same year. The second blow was the passing of my grandmother—my father's mother.

This particular loss was deeply resonant and complex. Its intensity stemmed not from decades of shared history, but from the fact that our relationship had a relatively short, yet extraordinarily meaningful, duration. Our connection was unique because I had only met this grandmother for the very first time when I was eighteen years old.

I had spent my childhood knowing about her, but circumstances had kept us apart. Finally meeting her was like discovering a missing piece of my personal history, a sudden injection of familial love and understanding that was warm, comforting, and long overdue. We quickly made up for lost time, building a foundation of affection and shared stories that felt ancient, though it was newly built.

Her passing was the abrupt and painful closing of a chapter that, though recently opened and all too brief, had already proven to be irreplaceable in the fabric of my identity. Losing her so soon after finding her amplified the grief, leaving a void where a burgeoning relationship had just begun to flourish.

One year later, the phone rang, delivering the news that tore another piece out of my soul: my sister Keisha had succumbed to the same brutal fate. Cancer. It felt like an awful, cruel repetition of history.

Another funeral service. Another service hat.

Losing Keisha was the first time I nearly regretted my decision to join the military. That sense of duty, of purpose, which had felt so absolute, suddenly felt like a terrible theft. I had only truly met her when I turned eighteen, a fleeting moment of connection before I shipped out. She was vibrant, funny, and full of life, and just as I was getting to know the person behind the title of "sister," I was gone.

That time away, those years spent training and deploying, could have been bonding time—a precious, irreplaceable chance to build a relationship with my sibling. Instead, they were years measured in distant phone calls and hurried, unsatisfying leave periods.

Now, looking at her casket, all those lost moments pressed down on me with the weight of a thousand regrets. I had chosen service over family, and the price of that choice felt utterly unbearable. I had left after just meeting her, and now she was gone forever. The weight of that absence, and the finality of it, settled deep in my chest.

The stories had always been there—whispered warnings, hushed anxieties—from my dad and my older brother Nate. They spoke of a creeping darkness they couldn't quite name, something happening with Donnie. But I had always managed to push them away. Sometimes I simply didn't believe the severity of what they were suggesting; other times, the truth felt too heavy, too complex for a person like me, immersed in the structured chaos of military life, to accept.

Something, undeniably, was happening to him—a shift in his mental landscape that was becoming increasingly pronounced to those around him. When I came home on leave, I'd make sure we hung out. Looking back, I can see how oblivious I was, or perhaps how effective he was at masking it. I genuinely didn't notice anything "crazy" during those visits. Sure, he'd grown a little distant over the years, the easy camaraderie of our youth replaced by a subtle barrier. But I rationalized that away. That was just life, wasn't it? The inevitable pull of careers, new routines, and separate geographies that chipped away at close family bonds.

Then came the moment that shattered my comfortable denial and forced me to confront the reality I had been avoiding. It was Keisha's funeral—our big sister, gone too soon. The whole family was there, a somber, tight-knit cluster of grief, except for the one person who should have been standing shoulder-to-shoulder with us: Donnie.

His absence was a gaping, screaming hole in the gathering, a betrayal that no reasonable excuse could cover. That's when the facts became undeniable: something profound and deeply troubling was going on with my brother.

After that day, he became a ghost. It wasn't just a matter of him missing a call or two; he became incredibly hard for me to get in touch with. My calls went unanswered. My texts were left on 'read' for days, sometimes a week. When he did reply, the messages were curt, vague, and devoid of his usual warmth, filled with hollow promises to "call you later."

It was a pattern of withdrawal that spoke louder and more clearly than any of the initial warnings from my dad or Nate. My brother was lost, and I was only just beginning to realize how far out of reach he had drifted.

Unbeknownst to me, while my sister Keisha spent her last days in the hospital before she succumbed to cancer, my dad was going through the exact same horrific ordeal. I honestly never saw it coming. My dad, Nate White—the one I affectionately called Pops —was the picture of health. He worked out religiously, maintained a rigorous daily routine, and seemed invincible. He was a man who embodied vitality, making his sudden diagnosis all the more shocking and bewildering.

But I guess a lifetime of being healthy isn't a reliable defense against The Big C. It strikes without prejudice.

The progression was tragically swift. Shortly after his 63rd birthday in January, my dad was placed in hospice care. Just seven agonizing days later, he left this Earth. The void he left was immediate and immense, a silent testament to the man who had been my bedrock.

In the midst of the fresh grief, my mind involuntarily flashed back to a conversation we had shared years earlier, in 2007. It was a raw, explosive moment that followed the shooting of my brother Nate. That day, fueled by years of suppressed pain and confusion, I yelled at him. I had confronted him about keeping me a secret, about the choice he made to keep me away from the rest of my family for so long. The words I threw at him were harsh, unforgiving, and saturated with accumulated anger.

Standing over his casket, a wave of regret threatened to drown me, but strangely, I couldn't completely surrender to it. Yes, I had exchanged sharp, unforgiving words with him. Yes, I had gotten a tremendous amount of pent-up anger off my chest that day. But that bitter, difficult confrontation was, paradoxically, the moment that truly brought us closer together. It was the moment that removed the metaphorical elephant from the room—a massive, silent weight of unaddressed history that had poisoned our relationship for years.

The things that needed to be addressed between us were finally confronted, no matter how uncomfortable the truth was. We laid it all bare, which allowed us to clear the path forward, a path we were able to walk together with true love and honesty in the years that followed. That fight wasn't the end; it was the necessary, painful beginning of a genuine connection.

And yet, despite the family tragedy and the profound sense of loss that had swept through us, my brother Donnie was noticeably, frustratingly absent from my father's funeral, just as he had been from Keisha's. His absence was a heavy, familiar echo of a deeper fracture that still ran through our family, a wound that seemed determined not to heal.

It was a year later—a year that marked another irreversible loss. But this subsequent death felt different, sharper, perhaps because it was inescapable for the one who had to attend. Donnie had no choice but to be present at this final gathering.

It was his own funeral.

Just mere weeks before, a different kind of grief had settled over my family. My Uncle Johnnie, a son from my granddad's life before he married my grandma, had passed away on my mother's side of the family. The day we were meant to lay Uncle Johnnie to rest became interwoven with another tragedy. It was the same evening that my little sister Crystal called me, her voice thick with the news about Donnie.

The sheer velocity of emotion that struck me was paralyzing. My thoughts didn't just race; they collided—a million chaotic fragments shattering the stillness of the day. The most profound, gutwrenching realization was the truth that I had never truly gotten the chance to sit down with him, man-to-man, and talk about whatever silent battle he was fighting. That unfinished conversation, that void of understanding, hit me with a crushing weight.

There was no closure, only a mountain of agonizingly unanswered questions—questions so complex, so profound, that they hadn't even had the time to fully form themselves in my shock-addled mind.

A single, haunting question, one I had often posed to myself in moments of quiet reflection, took on a brutal and terrifying new significance: *What if I had never become a Navy SEAL?*

The trajectory of my entire adult life seemed to hinge on this single career choice. If I had never joined the military, if I had stayed home right after he got out of the service, would we have had those precious, stolen years together? Would that additional time have been enough?

A relentless, self-incriminating cycle began: Is there any choice, any path I could have chosen, that would have somehow prevented my brother's death?

Donnie's funeral became a grim, final punctuation mark on a chapter of my life. It was the very last casket—the final symbol of a devastating loss—in which I would place one of my formal service hats, a SEAL trident prominently displayed, while I was still an active member of the military.

It was my final gesture of a brother's love and

a SEAL's farewell.

CHAPTER 12

Then Everything Went Black

It seemed like an endless cycle. From the moment I traded in my active duty uniform for the SEAL Reserves, the funerals began stacking up, year after relentless year. The gravity of loss often felt overwhelming, a heavy counterweight to the life I was building.

But even amidst the somber procession of so many deaths, life, in its vibrant and insistent way, offered moments of genuine joy. I was deeply honored to attend a host of weddings within the extended family, celebrations that served as necessary punctuation marks of hope and continuity.

My cousin Ann, on my father's side, was one of the first. She sent me an invitation to her wedding, but the timing was a bittersweet twist of fate. It arrived just two months after I had officially joined the Navy. I was literally still immersed in basic training when she was standing at the altar. It was a missed moment I often regretted.

However, I was able to make it to a truly significant family event in 2011: my dad's wedding. It was especially meaningful because the ceremony fell on his birthday. He married Razz, the wonderful woman he had introduced me to just a year prior. It was a beautiful, intimate day that felt like a powerful affirmation of new beginnings for him.

The wedding of my cousin Tionne and his wife Qyanna followed a couple of years later. Tionne extended the invitation to me shortly after Big O's funeral in 2012. It was a reminder of how closely sorrow and happiness often run together in a family's history.

Then came 2017. My cousin Mike married a lovely woman named Marilyn. Their union was particularly special as they had already welcomed another generation into the family—my little cousin,

Mike the 3rd. It was at this wedding that I had a chance encounter that became a reconnection. It was the first time I had seen his childhood friend Shad since we were teens. We spent a good portion of the reception catching up, the conversation naturally gravitating toward the shared, complex world of military life.

But of all the celebrations I had attended, it was the wedding in 2019 that filled me with the deepest sense of pride. Watching my little brother Kenny marry his partner Jen was a moment that felt like a culmination of all the good things in our family. It was a pure, unadulterated moment of brotherly happiness, a powerful reminder that while the funerals kept coming, life always, always found a way to celebrate.

The air in the grand hall was thick with a mixture of nostalgia, reverence, and the promise of a new chapter. That time finally came. After two decades of unwavering commitment to the nation, including a defining ten-year tenure as an active-duty Navy SEAL, my military journey was concluding, and the horizon of retirement beckoned.

Choosing the location for this pivotal moment was easy: my family's deep roots in Cincinnati meant that holding the retirement ceremony there would allow the maximum number of loved ones to attend and share in the day.

One of the most meaningful personal contributions I was able to make was the creation of my own presentation video. My extensive Audio-Video skills, honed over years of documenting missions and personal experiences, proved invaluable. I meticulously curated a powerful visual narrative, using a substantial amount of my own personally recorded footage. More significantly, I secured and incorporated approved footage from nearly all of my deployments across the globe. To round out the story of my service, I also included evocative clips from the grueling mental and physical crucible of SEAL training, and even the foundational days of basic training. The resulting film was a deeply personal testament to the chapters of my life in uniform.

The guest list was expansive, a reflection of the many communities that had sustained me over the years. Naturally, I invited virtually my entire extended family—my primary support structure. Beyond celebrating my own service, I felt a profound need to integrate a special tribute into the ceremony. This tribute was dedicated not only to the brave comrades I had lost in service—the brothers who never came home—but also to the cherished family members who had passed away along the way, whose memory I carried into every deployment and back.

The ceremony itself was steeped in the rich tradition and solemnity of the United States Navy. A flawlessly synchronized Honor Guard presented the U.S. flag in a precision maneuver as the soaring, powerful notes of the "National Anthem" filled the room, bringing every attendee to attention. A Chaplain offered the opening thoughts, centering the proceedings with a moment of spiritual reflection and gratitude.

Next, an official narrator stepped forward to read the formal retirement orders aloud.

The most poignant moment came when the audience stood at rigid attention as the final, official order relieving me from active duty was formally proclaimed. It was the sound of a twenty-year commitment being honorably fulfilled.

Following this, I was presented with two highly distinguished decorations: the Meritorious Service Medal and the Legion of Merit, both awarded for my exemplary performance and leadership during my final tour of duty. The formality concluded with the presentation of my official Certificate of Retirement and a highly prized Letter of Appreciation, signed by the Commander-in-Chief himself, U.S. President Biden.

It was a perfect, emotional capstone to a career dedicated to service.

Because I became a Reservist in my final seven years of service, the transition back to civilian life was surprisingly smooth and relatively easy. It wasn't the jarring cultural shift that so many veterans experience. I had already dipped my toes back into the civilian world, making the full plunge feel less like a shock and more like a gentle return to shore.

Three comfortable years had passed in this new, quiet chapter. I was sitting in the sun-drenched living room of my newly built home in Cincinnati, the silence broken only by the low hum of the air conditioning. It was a stark contrast to the constant, high-stakes operational tempo of my previous life.

In a moment of quiet reflection, an old military commercial—one I hadn't thought about in years—flashed through my memory. The commercial began with a provocative question: "If somebody wrote a book about your life, would anybody want to read it?"

The question hung in the air for only a second before I immediately thought, *Hell yeah somebody would want to read it.*

My life wasn't just a collection of anecdotes; it was a testament to transformation, discipline, and survival. I've read plenty of compelling books written by veterans, stories that resonated deeply because they captured the raw, uncompromising experience of elite service. I had devoured David Goggins' powerful memoirs, *Can't Hurt Me* and *Never Finished*, which offered an unfiltered look at mental toughness. I respected Marcus Luttrell's *Lone Survivor*, a visceral account of Operation Red Wings, and, of course, I admired *American Sniper* by the legendary Chris Kyle. My own journey, I felt, deserved its place among those narratives.

But what would I name my book?

The title had to be just right—capturing the essence of my journey without sounding cliché. For weeks, I rifled through an endless stream of possible titles, scribbling ideas on napkins and the backs of envelopes. At one point, I even thought about naming it after my self-given moniker from my SEAL days: *Jason The M.O.N.S.T.E.R.* I liked the grit of it, but I quickly dismissed the idea, realizing it sounded more like the title of a horror novel. It didn't translate the intended meaning, which was an acronym—Military Operations Navy SEAL Trained Elite Recon. The nuance was lost on a civilian audience.

The true moment of clarity arrived unexpectedly while I was driving. I was cruising down Interstate 75 in my black Hummer I had since my military days, navigating the familiar concrete ribbons of Cincinnati, and had to take the Western Avenue exit. That exit was a gateway to a lifetime ago; it was the location of the Cincinnati Job Corps center.

Seeing that unremarkable, blocky building—the place that had been my last stop before the military—brought back a flood of old memories and emotions. The pivotal realization hit me with the force of a physical blow: If it wasn't for that place, for that initial push toward structure and opportunity, I probably would have never even made the decision to join the military, much less become a Navy SEAL.

Then, the final piece of the puzzle clicked into place. I remembered the single, recurring, profound question that I had asked myself countless times throughout my career, from the grueling weeks of BUD/S training to the most intense moments of deployment. I realized that this question—my constant internal dialogue—should be the title of the book.

I must have contemplated this question a thousand times, and yet, in that moment on the highway, this would be the last time I'd ever ask it.

With a feeling of absolute certainty, I decided to name my book: *What If I Never Became a Navy SEAL?*

I must have zoned out in that intense moment of realization, letting my mind drift from the road as I processed the gravity of the decision. The silence in my car was suddenly shattered. All I heard was a violently loud, prolonged horn blast, a sound that cut through the quiet air like a knife.

I snapped my head up, my military training instantly trying to catch up to the danger, but it was too late. A massive, blue-and-white Cincinnati Metro bus was bearing down on me, its sheer mass dominating my windshield, moving straight and fast.

Then everything went black.

CHAPTER 13

Through the Sliding Doors

The rhythmic, intrusive beeping of hospital monitors was the first sensation to pierce the thick veil of unconsciousness. It wasn't pleasant—just an insistent, synthetic pulse that invaded the darkness of my mind.

Am I dead?

The thought was sharp, cold, and immediate. The absolute silence and blackness I'd been adrift in had given way to this sterile, electronic cacophony.

No, I can't be dead, another, more rational part of me countered. *If I were truly gone, I wouldn't be able to process that thought, to hear this noise, to feel... anything. The beeping and the distant hum of machinery were proof of existence, however tenuous. And it definitely wouldn't sound like I'm in a hospital.*

The scent of antiseptic—a sharp, clean odor that prickled my nose—confirmed the environment even before my eyes struggled to open.

A wave of intense, dull throbbing registered across my body, centered acutely in my head and ribs. Pain. A terrible sensation, yet in that moment, it was a profound affirmation of life.

Wait. A sudden realization clicked into place, cutting through the haze of pain and confusion. *If I'm in a hospital, that means I survived the crash.*

A breath caught in my chest, ragged and shallow. The last thing I remembered was the sickening crunch of metal, the sudden violent lurch, and then nothing but crushing blackness.

Survival. The word echoed in the confined space of my skull, a small, fragile victory against a monumental failure. I had made it.

But the lingering question hung heavy and unspoken in the sterile air: *How? And what's the damage?*

I slowly attempted to move a finger, testing the limits of my broken body and shattered memory.

I managed to force one eye to slowly slit open, followed by the second, a painful, grating motion against dry sockets. The air in the room felt thick, tasting faintly of antiseptic and something metallic—like old blood. I blinked rapidly, trying to clear the haze, bracing myself for the sight of a familiar, stark white hospital room.

Once my eyes were fully open, the creeping realization hit: something was terribly, fundamentally wrong.

I was expecting the physical hallmarks of injury—the rigid discomfort of a cast encasing my broken leg, the tight pressure of bandages wrapped around my arms, perhaps the dull ache of stitches. Instead, what greeted me was much worse, much more disorienting than any visible trauma I could have imagined.

Absolute, overwhelming blurriness.

The ceiling above me was a shapeless, pale smudge. The walls dissolved into indistinct masses of color. My hands, when I tried to raise them, were fuzzy outlines, and the entire world had been reduced to a swimming, frustrating canvas of soft edges and ambiguous light.

It wasn't just poor vision; it was a profound, nauseating lack of focus, as if the connection between my eyes and my brain had been severed. Panic began to prickle beneath my skin, a cold, sharp dread far more immediate than the memory of the crash that put me here.

Where am I? And why can't I see?

I had given up, eyes closed, hoping for a mental reset when a doctor finally entered the room.

"Can you hear me?"

I strained to open my eyes, wishing for clearer sight, but the blur remained. The words were in my head, yet when I tried to speak, only meaningless sounds escaped—a language without rhythm.

Unable to speak, I tried to form a word, but none would come out. The doctor, seeing my struggle, began a series of questions and commands to assess my comprehension.

"Can you tell me your name?" he asked. "Do you know where you are right now? Do you know what year it is?"

He followed up with tasks: "Can you squeeze my hand? Can you wiggle your toes for me? Hold up two fingers. Open your eyes really wide."

Finally, he asked, "Do you remember what happened?"

After nearly ten minutes of effort, I managed to force out a single word: "Bus."

"Impressive," the doctor commented, probing further. "What do you recall about the bus?"

"It hit me."

A flicker of confusion crossed the doctor's face. "It hit you? Are you saying a bus hit you?"

Shaking my head slowly, I finally managed to speak after a few minutes.

"Let's start with your name. Can you tell me your name?" the doctor asked.

"Jason," I replied slowly.

"Very good," the doctor said, his excitement rising at my level of awareness. "Jason, do you remember the year we're in?"

"25," I responded.

"I'll take that," the doctor confirmed.

"Do you know where you are?" he inquired.

"The hospital."

"Do you recall your arrival at the hospital?"

"Last night."

A slight smile crossed his face as he responded, "I can understand why you would assume that."

His reply indicated that my hospitalization had likely extended beyond a single night; however, to me, it felt as though I had awakened only hours after the incident. Nothing in my years of military service could have prepared me for his subsequent revelation.

"Mr. White, the year is 2026."

"2026?" I repeated, bewildered.

"Nevertheless, you were admitted to the hospital in 2025, which explains your assumption regarding the current year."

I remained silent, expressing only a series of confused expressions. He then leaned in closer.

"You have been in a coma for a year."

My immediate thought was that he was joking, but I quickly realized that in a serious time and place like this, such unprofessional joking would be entirely inappropriate for a doctor. Regardless, I still found myself hoping it was just a joke.

"Very funny," I groggily replied.

The persistent blurriness of my vision remained a concern, which could potentially be attributed to a year-long coma; thus, the possibility that he was not being facetious had to be considered.

"A year, huh? Does that explain why I can barely see?"

"Yes, that could be, or it could be the fact that you're not wearing your glasses," he replied, reaching by my bedside for a pair that had been there the whole time.

"Here, let me help you." He placed the pair of unfamiliar glasses on my face.

"How's that, better?"

"Yeah, it actually is, but now I'm even more confused."

Upon the moment the glasses were situated upon my nose, the world snapped into sharp, vibrant focus—a disorienting shock. The profound clarity momentarily eclipsed the alarming context: the year was 2026, and I had been in a coma for twelve months.

My mind fixated on the miracle of the custom-designed glasses. They fit uncannily, perfectly calibrating my vision, transforming the indistinct world into one of hyper-real detail. The sharp hospital tray table, the blanket fibers, the bedside cabinet's wood grain —all exploded into existence, pulling my focus from the lost time to the immediate, tangible reality of my recovered sight.

Undeniably, these glasses belonged to me. Yet, how? I was compelled to ask the most obvious question—obvious, that is, to him, but confusing to me.

"Whose glasses are these?"

Looking confused, the doctor replied, "Yours, correct? They arrived with you."

"But I don't wear prescription glasses," I persisted. "Before the accident, my vision was fine. A year-long coma could explain my deteriorating eyesight—I could understand that, I suppose—but the fact that this pair belongs to me is what's truly confusing."

"Mr. White, I understand this is likely confusing, but let's go back and discuss the accident that led to you being here. You mentioned a bus was involved, correct?"

"Yes, a bus hit me head-on."

"Do you recall the type of bus?"

"It was a Cincinnati Metro bus."

"So a Metro bus hit you head-on. What vehicle were you in at the time?"

"I was driving my black Hummer. It must be totaled, I assume?"

"Well, this might add to your confusion, but no black Hummer was involved. The only vehicle in the accident was the Metro bus." He paused briefly. "The one you were driving. Jason, you were driving the bus."

"I'm completely dumbfounded," I admitted. "I don't understand. Why would I be driving a Metro bus?"

"From what I understand, it's your job," he replied.

"I don't drive for Metro," I insisted. "But if, for some reason, I was behind the wheel of one of their buses, the crash would make sense because I don't know how to drive them."

The doctor continued, explaining the cause: "While you were driving the bus, you had a heart attack. That's what caused you to lose control and crash. It happened on the highway, and you crashed into a guardrail. There were no other vehicles involved."

I struggled to assemble the confusing pieces of this puzzle.

"So, you're telling me that back in 2025 I was working as a bus driver? That I had a heart attack, crashed, and just woke up in 2026?" I shook my head in disbelief. "And on top of all that... now I wear glasses?"

"It says right here that you work for Metro and that you were on the clock during the accident," the doctor said. "So, Jason, help me understand—if you don't work for Metro, what do you do for a living?"

"Currently? I'm a Real Estate Agent," I said. "But I'm also a retired

Navy SEAL."

The doctor remained silent, studying me with a look of bewildered interest.

"I spent twenty years in the military," I added, trying to clarify.

The doctor cut in. "The military? Retired Navy SEAL?" He glanced back at his notes. "Well... that is certainly news to me."

The doctor probed further. "So, what year did you retire?"

"2022," I insisted, the dates rolling off my tongue like a cadence I'd recited a thousand times.

"I joined the Navy in 2002, completed SEAL training in 2005, spent ten years as an active SEAL until 2015, and served as a Reservist until my retirement in 2022." I gestured toward his clipboard. "And you mean to tell me none of this is in your notes?"

He glanced down at the chart, then back at me. "No," the doctor said gently. "Jason, your background shows no military history whatsoever."

The words hung in the air, heavy and suffocating.

"What the fuck," I mumbled to myself.

"There must be some kind of mistake," I pleaded. "Is there another Jason you might be confusing me with?"

The thought sparked a flicker of hope. Maybe this was just a clerical error.

"Administrative errors happen," the doctor admitted. "But a mixed-up file wouldn't explain the glasses sitting on your face right now."

He was right. No amount of shuffled paperwork could explain why prescription lenses fit me perfectly. The tiny flame of hope was snuffed out instantly.

"Jason, let me ask you this," he continued, shifting tactics. "You stated that before the crash, you didn't need corrective lenses. Is that correct?"

"Technically, yes," I clarified. "I needed them in high school. But before I joined the Navy, I got LASIK surgery. I had to do it to qualify for SEAL training."

"So, you haven't always had perfect vision. At some point in your life, you did wear glasses?"

"Yes." I paused, correcting myself. "Well, mostly contacts in high school. Glasses were more of an elementary school thing."

"I'm just trying to establish a timeline here," he said, leaning in. "So, up until high school, you remember needing corrective lenses to see? You're sure of that?"

"Yes."

"And what year did this LASIK surgery take place?"

"2002."

"Was that immediately after high school?"

"Not exactly. I had just completed the Cincinnati Job Corps program." I felt the need to explain further. "I didn't graduate traditional high school. I enrolled in Job Corps, finished that, and then got the surgery right before enlisting."

"Got it," the doctor replied, looking back down at his notes.

"Let's just verify that you are the same Jason I have in my paperwork."

He glanced at the clipboard, then leveled his gaze at me.

"We have already established that your name is Jason White, correct?"

"Correct."

"Middle name?"

"D'Marlo."

"That matches what I have here," he noted, checking a box. "Date of birth?"

"Twelve-thirty, eighty-two."

"Yup, that checks out as well. And your social security number?"

I rattled off the digits.

Once he confirmed the number, the last sliver of doubt evaporated. The person in his paperwork—the bus driver who had a heart attack—was undeniably me.

"My clipboard only covers the basics," the doctor explained. "I'm going to step out and grab my laptop. That way, we can take a deeper look at your history and hopefully jog your memory."

"Okay," I said, the word feeling hollow.

"And while I'm gone, I'll call your family to let them know you've awakened. Seeing them might be exactly what you need to ground yourself."

"Sounds good."

As soon as the door clicked shut, the silence rushed back in, and my mind started racing. I needed proof. I frantically scanned the room for a cell phone. A phone would be the smoking gun—photos of my platoon, texts to my commanding officer, contacts with call signs. It would prove I wasn't crazy.

I checked the bedside table, the rails, the sheets.

Nothing.

The door opened, and the doctor returned, flanked by a pair of nurses. He wheeled a laptop cart to the bedside, the screen glowing with what I assumed was the dossier of a stranger—my medical history.

For what felt like an eternity, he scrolled through a digital litany of visits I had no memory of. The flu. Minor injuries. Routine check-ups. None of it triggered a spark of recognition.

Then, his scrolling stopped.

"May, 2013." He read the date, then looked up over the rim of his glasses, his expression grave.

A knot formed in my stomach. "What's wrong?" I asked, hesitating. "Why was I in the hospital then?"

"Let me ask you this first: have you ever struggled with depression?"

"No, not really," I said defensively. "I mean... back when my grandma died, I took it hard. I kind of shut down, stopped doing schoolwork. That's actually why I was pulled out of school and put into Job Corps in the first place. But that was back in 1994 when I was eleven years old. You're talking about 2013—nearly twenty years later."

The doctor didn't blink.

"The reason I ask about depression, Jason, is because you were admitted in May of 2013 for a suicide attempt."

The room went dead silent. He didn't rush to elaborate; he just let the weight of the statement settle over me.

I stared at him, my brain stalling out, unable to process the words.

"Suicide?" I mumbled, the word tasting like ash in my mouth.

The doctor's voice finally broke the heavy silence.

"Does hearing that shock you, Mr. White?"

"Shock me?" I let out a harsh, disbelief-filled breath. "At first, I was expecting you to tell me I'd been shot or something. Even when you asked about depression, suicide didn't even cross my mind." I shook my head, trying to reconcile this stranger's life with my own memories. "If this is real... what the fuck was going on with me in 2013?"

I looked him dead in the eye. "I would never try to kill myself. I spent an entire career killing others."

Realizing how unhinged that sounded in a hospital room, I quickly clarified. "I mean targets. Enemy combatants I was ordered to engage in service to this country. That is the only killing I've ever done. I certainly wouldn't turn the weapon on myself."

"Wait, did I shoot myself?" My hands flew to my head, fingers frantically probing my scalp for the scar of a bullet wound.

"No," the doctor replied, glancing back at the screen. "It lists the method as a drug overdose. Apparently, you took a handful of pills."

The room fell into heavy silence, leaving me speechless.

Then, a sharp knock broke the tension, and five people walked in. All female. These had to be the people the doctor called when he briefly stepped out.

Three of them were complete strangers to me: a young woman in her late teens or early twenties, and two small children—a toddler and a baby who looked barely a year old.

The fourth woman was older, perhaps the mother of the first three. She looked vaguely familiar—a nagging sense of recognition I couldn't quite place—but I couldn't attach a name to the face.

The fifth person, however, I knew instantly. My mother.

As soon as they crossed the threshold, the toddler wasted no time. She bolted toward my bedside.

"Daddy! Daddy!" Her voice was shrill with excitement, her face beaming with pure, unadulterated joy.

I froze. I didn't have children. I had never laid eyes on this little girl before in my life. But looking at her, there was no doubt—she knew me, and she knew me as her father.

The doctor stayed silent for a moment, carefully observing the interaction between the toddler and me, before finally stepping in.

"Welcome back," he said, nodding to the group that had just entered.

My mom remained quiet, standing near the back, but she was smiling—relief washing over her face to see me awake. To my surprise, it was the familiar-looking woman who spoke up first.

"So, how is he doing?" she asked, her voice tight with nerves, clearly not knowing what to expect.

"Well, I'm still trying to gauge his level of consciousness," the doctor replied cautiously. "There seems to be something going on with his memory that I can't quite pinpoint."

"What are you saying?" she pressed. "Does he have amnesia or something?"

"Not exactly. It doesn't seem like his memory was erased." He paused for a beat, choosing his words carefully. "It seems more like it was... replaced."

"Kind of like a glitch in his reality." He continued.

"Replaced?" she repeated, confusion wrinkling her brow.

The doctor turned back to me. "Mr. White, do you recognize any of the people who just walked in?"

"Yeah," I replied instantly. "That's my mom."

"Okay, that's a good sign." He gestured toward the woman who had spoken. "What about her?"

I stared at her, the features clicking into place as a specific memory surfaced through the haze.

"Wait... I do remember you," I said slowly. "Torri, right?"

"Yes!" she breathed out, her face lighting up. She looked visibly relieved that I knew her name.

"That's excellent," the doctor said, encouraged. "And do you know who Torri is?"

"Yeah, but... I'm a bit confused as to why she's here."

Torri's smile faltered, transforming into a look of bewilderment.

The doctor leaned in. "Why is Torri's presence confusing, Mr. White?"

"I mean, I know her, but we aren't close," I explained, looking between them. "I met her at a family reunion on my dad's side, back around 2015. We were introduced by our cousins, Rally and Christina. We talked for a bit because she looked familiar—we realized we went to the same high school and shared a mutual friend. But that was it. That's as far as it went."

The room went dead silent.

The doctor turned to Torri. "Is that correct? Is that how you two met?"

"That is not how we met," Torri whispered, the color draining from her face as the doctor's theory about "replaced" memories suddenly made terrifying sense. "But we did meet in 2015, though. That part is correct."

"Okay, you mentioned something earlier about his memory being replaced," my mom said, finally breaking her silence. "What exactly did you mean by that?"

"Jason and I spoke for quite a while before you arrived," the doctor replied, addressing the room. "And it appears that the objective facts of his history are completely at odds with his personal recollections."

He paused, letting the weight of the diagnosis hang in the air before elaborating.

"It's almost as if he remembers living a completely different life."

"Different how?" Torri interjected, her voice sharp.

The doctor turned to me, offering a subtle nod. "Well, Jason, the floor is yours."

I shifted my attention to the most familiar face in the room—the one person I knew wouldn't lie to me.

"Mom, please tell me," I pleaded. "Didn't I retire from the military?"

She stared at me blankly, total confusion washing over her face. The word *military* hung in the air between us like a foreign object —alien, unrecognized, and completely out of place.

"A Navy SEAL," I insisted.

The specific title seemed to spark a memory in my mom. She began to nod her head slowly, igniting the flare of hope I had been desperately searching for.

"Yes," she said. "You used to talk about becoming a Navy SEAL all the time... back when you were in Job Corps."

The doctor immediately interjected. "So, he did attend Job Corps?"

He quickly scribbled the confirmation into his notes, validating the timeline but not the career.

"And he had plans to become a Navy SEAL at that time?" the doctor pressed.

"Yes," my mom answered. She turned her gaze to me, her eyes filled with pity. "But that's as far as it went. When you were kicked out of Job Corps, that Navy SEAL dream died then."

She paused, then drove the point home. "Because you didn't have your GED when you were kicked out, so you couldn't go to the military anyway."

Hearing the word *dream* triggered a sudden realization—a potential explanation that actually made sense.

My mind flashed back to the seconds before the crash. I remembered the specific thought occupying my mind right before the metal crunched: the title of my book. The one question I had always asked myself.

What if I never became a Navy SEAL?

That was the last thing I thought, then came the crash, and immediately after, I woke up here.

Maybe this is the universe's way of showing what that life is like.

A wave of relief washed over me. That had to be it. I'm still in a coma from the accident, and this... this is just a dream. This is the universe's way of answering my question, showing me exactly what that life would have looked like.

But even as I clung to that theory, a cold doubt crept in. This felt too solid. Too vivid. It felt more real than any dream I've ever had.

Before I could challenge the Job Corps story, the toddler demanded attention again.

"Daddy! Daddy! Mommy, see Daddy?" she squealed, trying to scramble up the side of the hospital bed.

"So, you really don't know who she is?" Torri asked softly, moving to help the little girl up onto the mattress.

I just shook my head, staring at the child who was looking at me with total adoration.

"But if I had to guess," I said, looking between them, "I would say she's our child. Are all three of these girls ours?"

"Yes... well, mostly," Torri corrected herself.

She gestured to the toddler now sitting beside me. "Natalie," she said, then reached down to lift the one-year-old from her carrier, "and Jayla... are the kids we have together."

She then pointed toward the teenager standing awkwardly near the door.

"Talia," she explained, "is your oldest. She has a different mother."

"So... Talia, Natalie, and Jayla?" I repeated the names, my voice thick with a strange mix of confusion and unexpected excitement. *I actually had kids.*

I pointed to Torri. "And Natalie and Jayla are ours? But Talia has a different mother?"

"Yes," Torri confirmed softly.

I turned my full attention to Talia, the adult stranger who was apparently my daughter.

"So, how old are you?"

"Twenty-two," she replied, offering a nervous chuckle, though her eyes remained serious.

I looked away, muttering the number to myself. "Twenty-two..."

The gears in my head began to grind, trying to overlay her age onto my military timeline.

"What year were you born?"

"2004."

2004. I would have been deep in training then.

"I'm almost afraid to ask," I hesitated, "but who is your mother?"

"My mom's name is Shana."

"Do you know when or how we met?"

"I think you told me something about the Black Family Reunion," she said, furrowing her brow as she tried to recall the story I'd apparently told her. "In 2000 or 2001? Something like that."

"Shana... Black Family Reunion... 2001," I whispered to myself.

The room went quiet, everyone watching me intently, waiting to see if this specific combination of facts would finally unlock some kind of memory.

Talia tapped on her screen, searching for a photo, then thrust the phone toward me.

I stared at the image for a solid ten seconds, the face slowly dredging up a memory I hadn't touched in decades. Then, it clicked.

"Shana!" I looked up, shocked. "From the Black Family Reunion in 2001? That's your mother?!"

Before she could confirm, the doctor cut in. "So, you do recognize her?" He poised his pen over his clipboard, ready to record the connection.

"Yes," I admitted. "But the timeline doesn't make sense. I only knew her for about nine months before I shipped out for the Navy in 2002." I looked at Talia, shaking my head. "I mean, we were close, sure. But we never... we never did anything."

"Regardless of the details," the doctor noted, "the fact that you know who she is is extremely important."

"Is that everyone? Is this all the children we have?" I asked, looking up at Torri.

"There's one more," she smiled. "I have a son named Lawrence. We call him Bubbie."

"So, I have a stepson?" I asked, a grin spreading across my face. "How are we? Do we get along?"

"Absolutely," Torri said without hesitation. "Actually, you guys are tight. He works at Metro with you."

"Really? We work together?"

"Yes, and it doesn't stop there. You two also shoot pool on a team together with your cousin Kenny."

"I'm in a pool league?" I laughed, trying to picture it. "With Lil'

Kenny?"

"Yes. And a bowling league, too."

"I bowl in a league?" I looked at my hands, imagining a bowling ball. "Am I actually any good?"

"Yes," she nodded assuredly. "You are."

Holding Talia's phone reminded me of my own missing lifeline.

"If I had my phone," I stammered, "maybe I could prove... or... show you something..." I couldn't find the words to finish the thought. I just needed access to my old life.

Torri reached into her purse and withdrew a device I didn't recognize.

"Will this help?" she asked, handing me what was apparently my phone.

It felt foreign in my hand—the weight was wrong, the case unfamiliar—but I tapped the screen awake anyway. I punched in my PIN, the same code I had used for fifteen years.

INCORRECT PIN.

The error message flashed on the screen, mocking me.

Torri noticed my hesitation. She gently took the phone from my hand, tapped in a quick sequence effortlessly, and handed it back.

Unlocked.

I stared at the open home screen, a cold realization settling in.

She knows the passcode.

In my life—my real life—I never gave anyone access to my phone. Strict operational security. I never gave that code to a soul, certainly not a woman.

But she knew it.

Scrolling through this device felt like invading the privacy of a complete stranger.

I checked the contacts first. The list was endless, but outside of a few family members, I didn't recognize a single name. Who were these people?

I switched to the gallery. It was filled with hundreds of photos I had no memory of taking, yet the evidence was undeniable. There I was—smiling, laughing, living a life I didn't know. Dozens of selfies of me and Torri, looking happy. Looking close.

Then, I opened the Facebook app and tapped on my profile. The cover photo stopped me cold.

It was me and Torri. Dressed in white. On our wedding day.

The shock hit me like a physical blow. Discovering we had kids was one thing; knowing she had my passcode was another. But marriage? I hadn't even considered that we were actually husband and wife.

I looked up from the screen, my gaze dropping instantly to her left hand.

Sure enough, there it was. A wedding band glinting in the hospital light. I couldn't believe I hadn't noticed it before.

I slowly raised my eyes to meet hers. The silence stretched between us. I couldn't even find my voice; I just mouthed the words: *We're married?*

She didn't answer immediately. Instead, she reached back into her purse and pulled out a matching band—my ring.

"You know, for the first four months, I left this on you," she explained softly, turning the platinum band between her fingers. "But you lost some weight lying in that bed. It kept slipping off and getting lost in the sheets."

She took my left hand in hers, her touch warm against my skin.

"I was terrified I'd lose it, so I started keeping it with me. I only put it back on when I'm here."

She slid the ring onto my finger. It settled into place with a weight that felt undeniable.

"Yes," she whispered, smoothing her thumb over the metal. "We're married."

"How long?" I asked, my voice barely a whisper.

"Not long. We got married in May of 2025," she explained gently. "The accident happened just five months later."

She paused, a sad smile touching her lips. "For your birthday that year, I had a trip planned. I was going to take you to Vegas. It was going to be a huge milestone—your first time on a plane."

"First time on a plane?" I repeated, the concept sounding absolutely ridiculous to me.

I looked at her like she was crazy.

"Torri, throughout my military career, I've been on hundreds of planes. I've jumped out of perfectly good aircraft at twenty thousand feet. And you're telling me I've never even stepped foot on a commercial flight?"

My frustration finally boiled over, spilling out in a desperate, frantic rant.

"Okay, this is seriously crazy," I snapped. "How come I don't remember any of what you all are talking about? How is it possible that I remember living a completely different life? I have specific memories! I remember getting LASIK right before I shipped out. Uncle Mike paid for it!"

I turned to my mother, begging her to validate just one detail.

"Mom, you don't remember that? I wrote you letters the whole time I was away. I have literally been around the world. I met four Presidents! I bought you Grandma's house on Woolper!"

The mention of the house made me pause. That was a huge achievement in my life—buying that home for her.

"So," I asked slowly, dreading the answer, "you're saying you don't live in Grandma's house?"

"I live downtown," she replied softly, shaking her head. "At Parktown. And so does Talia."

I frantically searched my memory for a tether to the real world—something verifiable, an event they could research but one where I knew the intimate details.

I thought about Chris Kyle. I trained with him, attended his funeral. But he was too famous; knowing about him didn't prove I was a SEAL, just that I watched the news. I needed something personal.

Then I thought of JT. And his dog.

"Jon Tumilson!" I blurted out.

The room stared at me in confusion.

"Go on YouTube," I commanded, pointing at Talia. "Look up 'Navy SEAL funeral dog.'"

Talia frowned, her thumbs hovering over her screen. "What? Since when do dogs have funerals?"

"No, listen to me," I urged. "My friend JT was a Navy SEAL. At his funeral, his dog walked up to the casket and laid down right in front of it for the entire service. He wouldn't leave him. The video is out there. Find it."

Talia typed in the search terms. A moment later, she pressed play. Everyone gathered around the small screen, watching the two-minute clip of the heartbreaking scene.

"Now," I said, looking at their faces. "Even if that video is on YouTube, how would I even know to look for it? I'm pretty sure there was no news coverage about that in Cincinnati back in 2011. He was from Iowa."

I scanned the room. "Before right now, did anyone here know that video existed?"

Silence. No one said a word.

Then, a realization hit me. I had another weapon in my arsenal. A skill that couldn't be faked.

"Hasta ahora, ¿alguien aquí sabía que existía ese vídeo?"

The words flowed out of me effortlessly—perfect, fluent Spanish.

Everyone froze, looking at me in confused amazement. They looked like they weren't sure if I was speaking a foreign language or speaking in tongues.

I locked eyes with Torri.

"Can the Jason you married speak Spanish?"

Torri shook her head slowly, her eyes wide with a mixture of fear and awe. She was stunned.

"Babe, look... I honestly don't know what to think right now," Torri said, reaching out to grip my hand tight. "But I do know this. The life you described sounds like a wonderful life. But in this life, you are a family man. A loving father and an amazing husband."

She squeezed my hand, urging me to look away from her and back at the children.

"Just look at your girls. Look at how they light up when they see you."

I decided to shift the focus, needing more visual proof.

"Do you have any other wedding photos on your phone?"

Torri opened her Google Photos gallery and handed the device over to me.

There were over nine hundred photos. I spent the next hour scrolling through them, absorbing every detail of a day I couldn't recall.

"Wow," I whispered, genuinely amazed at the production. "This looks like it was an incredible wedding. I really wish I could remember it."

Next, they showed me the videos—highlights of the wedding and family montages that I had apparently edited myself.

"You have an Audio/Video degree in this life," Torri reminded me gently. "You make all our family movies."

I watched the screen, mesmerized. The editing style was familiar —hauntingly so. These videos looked exactly like the projects I had been trying to create with my own home footage back in my other life, but I had never been able to get the flow right. I had the vision, but not the technical skill.

I guess, in this life, I knew exactly what to do.

As the weeks blurred by, a parade of family members came to visit. They offered well wishes, but their true mission was clear: they were trying to convince me of the life they said I lived, overlaying my memories with their stories.

Physical therapy became my new mission. After weeks of grueling work, I reached the point where I could finally walk again. But the mental recovery was even harder.

For weeks, I met with a neuropsychologist—sort of a detective for the brain. He didn't just talk to me; he interviewed my mom and Torri at length, cross-referencing their stories with the attending physician's notes.

Finally, after gathering all the evidence, they were ready.

The room felt small with everyone packed inside: the primary doctor, the neuropsychologist, my mom, Torri, and me. The air was thick with anticipation. They had come to a conclusion.

The neuropsychologist sat forward, a thick manila folder resting on his knees. It looked heavy—heavy enough to contain an entire life.

"Good afternoon, Mr. White," he began, his voice calm and professional. "After speaking with your family, I've done some additional research into your history to try and reconcile these conflicting timelines."

"What kind of research?" I asked, bracing myself.

"Well, there were anchor points in both 'lives' that were similar, but the outcomes were different. Take the GED, for instance. You and your mother both agree that you attended Job Corps and that you failed the test on your first attempt. However, I contacted the State Department of Education and pulled your full testing history."

He opened the folder and pointed to a document.

"The first test was taken in 2001, just as you remembered at Job Corps. You failed. There was a second attempt in 2004. You failed that one as well. The official record shows that you didn't pass until 2011."

"2011?!" I blurted out, the shock turning inward. *Why the hell did I wait so long?*

"There were also discrepancies regarding your exit from Job Corps," he continued. "You claimed you completed the program in 2002. I obtained a copy of your records from the Cincinnati center. You were actually terminated from the program for disorderly conduct in 2001. Your mother was correct."

He flipped the page.

"There were other inconsistencies," the doctor continued, his tone shifting. "Specific details about your service that simply don't align with history."

"Like what?" I demanded. "I know where I was. I know who I served with."

"You mentioned meeting **Marcus Luttrell** in the chow hall in the summer of 2005," he said, reading from his notes. "You described him walking around, eating lunch, prepping for a deployment."

"Yeah," I said. "He was quiet. A ghost."

"Jason, in the summer of 2005, Marcus Luttrell was in a hospital bed recovering from massive trauma—shrapnel, a broken back, a shattered leg. He wasn't walking anywhere. He certainly wasn't prepping for a deployment."

He didn't wait for me to argue. He just moved to the next point.

"You also mentioned recovering on the **USS Bainbridge** after a mission in Somalia in early 2006. Is that correct?"

"Yes. We used it for decompression."

He shook his head slowly. "In early 2006, the *USS Bainbridge* wasn't in Somalia. It was still in the Atlantic doing workups. It didn't deploy to that region until 2007, and it didn't become famous for anti-piracy operations until the *Maersk Alabama* incident in 2009. You placed yourself on that specific ship because you've seen the movie *Captain Phillips*, not because you were actually there."

I opened my mouth to protest, but he cut me off with one final blow.

"And then there is **Chris Kyle**. You said you met him in Ramadi in the summer of 2007."

"I did," I insisted. "We trained together. He was already a legend."

"He *was* a legend," the doctor corrected. "But Chris Kyle's famous deployment to Ramadi—the one where he earned the nickname 'The Devil of Ramadi'—was in 2006. By the summer of 2007, he was back in the United States. You couldn't have met him in Ramadi then."

He closed the folder with a soft thud.

"Your mind is pulling facts from movies and books—*Lone Survivor*, *Captain Phillips*, *American Sniper*—and stitching them together to create a timeline that *feels* real, but falls apart under scrutiny."

"Finally, I reached out to the Department of Defense. I gave them your social security number and all your information."

"And?"

"Nothing came back, Jason. No DD-214. No service number. There is absolutely no record of you ever enlisting in the United States Armed Forces."

The room spun slightly. "Okay," I stammered, "then why do I only remember that reality? If I wasn't a SEAL, how do I know about JT's dog? How is it that I can speak Spanish now when I couldn't before?"

The neuropsychologist closed the folder and leaned in. "Jason, answer me this: When was the last time you had a dream?"

The question caught me off guard. I searched my mind, thinking back as far as I could.

"I... I don't know. Now that I think about it, I haven't had a dream in years. Well, besides this apparently being a dream, I haven't had one since before the military. Why does that matter?"

"You don't find it strange that you haven't had a dream in over two decades?"

"Yeah," I admitted. "That is weird. Why?"

"I'll explain. But first, with your permission, I looked into your digital footprint. Specifically, your media consumption."

"My what?"

"Your Amazon Prime and Audible accounts," he said. "Your watch history shows that you have binged the television series *SEAL*

Team, as well as the movies *Lone Survivor* and *American Sniper*. Your Audible library tells the same story. You've listened to the audiobooks for those titles, as well as David Goggins' *Can't Hurt Me* and *Never Finished*."

"Okay... but so what? I like military movies."

"Jason, do you know how dreams work?"

"People sleep, they dream. What's the point?"

"Dreams are the brain's way of processing data. They consolidate memories, transfer short-term thoughts to long-term storage, and simulate social situations. Usually, this happens in bursts throughout the night. But you were in a coma for a year. Your brain was active, but it had no external input. So, it turned inward."

He tapped the folder.

"You lived with one burning question your entire life: 'What If I became a Navy SEAL?' Your subconscious used that as the foundation. It took everything you've read, watched, and listened to about Navy SEALs and constructed a simulation so detailed, so visceral, that it overwrote your reality."

"But the dog..." I whispered.

"I've listened to David Goggins' book, *Can't Hurt Me*," the doctor said gently. "In it, he describes the funeral of Jon Tumilson and his dog in vivid detail. That is how you knew about it. Your brain visualized the story you heard."

"And the Spanish?"

"The mind is powerful. In your dream, you were a linguist. You believed it so fully that your brain unlocked the capability, perhaps mimicking phrases you'd heard in movies or songs, creating a phantom skill."

He sat back. "The reason you haven't had a dream since Job Corps is because, since the moment of the crash, you have been living inside one continuous, unbroken dream. And now, you've finally woken up."

I remained silent. The logic was airtight. There was no argument left to make.

The doctor's words about Job Corps stung. I had convinced myself that the military saved me. In my mind, the SEAL Teams had been the lifeboat that kept me from drowning in my own mistakes. I had failed public school. I had failed my first GED test. And now, according to the file on the doctor's lap, I had failed Job Corps, too.

"I joined the SEAL Team to save myself from being a failure," I said, my voice quiet, addressing the room but seeing only my past. "Because I had no plans otherwise."

I slowly turned my gaze to my mom, the weight of the diagnosis crushing me.

"So... I failed again, huh?"

"Jason, look around you," she started, her voice firm but gentle. "Look at all the family that came to visit you while you've been lying in this bed. You think you failed? Because of you, our family has precious videos of the most special moments in their lives. You created that legacy for them."

She leaned closer, making sure I heard every word.

"You graduated twice, Jason. You went back and got your GED, and then you graduated from Cincinnati State with a degree in Audio/ Video Production. Most people in our family only finished high school. But you pushed through college. You are more successful than you even know."

Torri leaned in, taking my hand again.

"Babe, you also have a family that absolutely adores you. Talia, Natalie, Jayla... you are their whole world."

My mom cut back in, nodding at her daughter-in-law. "And you have a wife most men could only wish for."

Torri squeezed my hand, holding my gaze. "So you tell me... does that look like the life of a failure?"

All I could do was smile. The logic was undeniable. They were right. I wasn't a failure; I was a success in ways I hadn't even realized. But as beautiful as it sounded, I couldn't shake the lingering feeling: This life was one I just didn't know.

I excused myself to the restroom, needing to be alone with my thoughts for a minute. I gripped the porcelain sink and stared into the mirror. I was looking for the Jason I knew—the warrior, the sailor.

For a split second, I saw him standing there in his white service uniform.

The same one I had worn at many of my family members' funerals.

Then, he blinked. And he disappeared forever.

A short time later, I was released.

I approached the exit. Through the glass, I saw a black Hummer drive slowly past the pickup lane, windows down, bass thumping. The song blasting from the speakers was unmistakable. It was Biggie Smalls' "Juicy."

Just as the glass panels began to part, the first five words of the first verse drifted in on the wind, a final message from the universe.

"It was all a dream."

The spell broke. The false memories evaporated, replaced instantly by the weight and truth of who I really was.

I walked out into the open air, and suddenly, I was free. I realized then that as long as I had been inside that building—the place that had conjured up that alternate reality—the memories of the SEAL would linger.

The fantasy was behind me the moment I stepped

through the sliding doors.

What if I never became a Navy SEAL?

That is a powerful, almost haunting question, isn't it? It's the "What If"—those two deceptively simple words—that injects the sentence with such profound emotional weight. The "what if" opens the door to an alternate reality, a life unlived, a path not taken. It represents a moment of reflection, a bittersweet glance back at a fork in the road where destiny hung in the balance.

But here is the stark, unvarnished truth; the cold reality that underpins this whole line of inquiry.

If you remove those two words—"What If"—from the beginning of the sentence, the powerful, hypothetical question collapses into a simple, undeniable statement of fact.

I never became a Navy SEAL.

The hypothetical scenario—the dream, the aspiration, the goal that dominated a definitive period of my life—did not materialize. That path was closed. The objective was not achieved. The uniform was never earned. This is the bedrock fact upon which all subsequent reflection must stand.

Life is full of 'what ifs'. Everyone has wrestled with them at some point. We are all faced with decisions every single day that render different outcomes. But you can only choose one. And whichever path you choose, you can't help but look over your shoulder and wonder about the road you left behind.

People often ask the internal questions: *What if I hadn't dropped out of school? What if I had finished my degree? What if I had stayed? What if I had left?*

But sometimes, the "what if" is more complex. It isn't always about a choice you made, but about a choice that was made for you. It's about the things out of your immediate control.

You may ask, *"What if I got that high-paying job I applied for?"* You did your part. You applied. You may have even crushed the interview. But ultimately, the decision was not in your hands. The door didn't open, not because you didn't knock, but because it was locked from the other side.

I think back to that specific day at Job Corps. The day the teacher decided to get smart with me, ending her sentence with a condescending, *"Duh."*

She made me feel small that day—and she was known for doing exactly that. I must have reached my boiling point. But instead of doing the smart thing—standing up and walking out of the classroom to cool off—I did the one thing I couldn't take back.

I stood up, got right in her face, and cussed her out. I didn't touch her, but I was close enough for her to say the magic words: *"I felt threatened."*

That one decision—to lash out in anger instead of keeping my cool—altered the trajectory of my entire life.

I was terminated from the program that same day. Zero tolerance. I never even got a chance to tell my side of the story. And sure, I had a point. A teacher should never talk to a student the way she did, basically calling them stupid. We were students, but we weren't children, and her level of respect for us was non-existent. I should have voiced that opinion through the proper channels. Instead, I gave them a reason to kick me out.

But then, I have to look deeper.

I was only in her class that day because I had failed the first GED test. If I had passed it, I would have moved on. I would have never been in her classroom that day, and never lost my spot.

Job Corps was my mother's lifeline—her last, desperate attempt to steer me onto the right track back then. She had pinned her hopes on me walking away with a GED and a trade, a foundation for a real life.

Instead, I came back empty-handed. Kicked out.

I was forced to move back into her house, not as a child, but as an adult with no education, no job, and absolutely no plan for the future.

At the time, I was too wrapped up in my own ways to see it. But looking back now, I realize I never stopped to consider how that failure must have made her feel.

When I walked away from Job Corps, I wasn't just leaving a campus; I was stepping out of the structure that had defined my entire existence.

For the first time since preschool, I wasn't a student. I wasn't a trainee. I wasn't part of any institution. I was just... out there. And for the first time, I felt truly alone.

Don't get me wrong—my mom was still in my corner. She helped me whenever she could. But the dynamic had shifted. She still had my little brother, Kenny, to raise. Her focus had to be on him, ensuring he got through high school and didn't fall off the path the way I just had.

Since the age of 15, I have cycled through roughly 40 different jobs. I've been everything from a line cook to a tow truck driver, and eventually, a bus driver. At one point, I even took a shot at building something of my own, starting a business as a freight broker.

Back in Job Corps, becoming a Navy SEAL wasn't just a fantasy; it was *the* plan. It was the first time I felt genuinely excited about my future. Had I followed through—even if I had just joined the regular military—there is no doubt I would have gained the discipline, structure, and skills that come with the uniform.

But in my young mind, the military felt like a "packaged deal" with Job Corps. Since the dream was born there, I felt like it had to stay there. When I got kicked out, I let the ambition stay behind.

For years, I tried to rationalize it. Especially after 9/11 changed the world. I knew that if I had become a SEAL, I would have been deploying into the heat of war. So I told myself lies to feel better. I'd say, "Man, I really dodged a bullet," or "Good thing I didn't go, Bush is just sending troops over there to die."

But deep down, I knew I was lying. I felt like I had strayed off the path I was meant to travel.

That unresolved regret is exactly why I cycled through so many jobs. I had no problem quitting good roles or failing to take work seriously, because a voice in my head kept whispering, *This isn't where you're supposed to be. You're meant for something more.*

I dwelled on that missing life so much that I failed to realize something crucial: I *was* learning. I *was* gaining skills. I just didn't see them because they didn't come with a trident.

Fast forward to 2011. Ten years later. I finally earned my GED at the age of 28. With that piece of paper in hand, I tried to rekindle the old flame.

I walked into a recruiter's office, chest out, and asked about becoming a SEAL.

Now, back in high school and Job Corps, recruiters were like sharks. They made it their business to sign up anyone with a pulse. But the guy I met that day? He had to be the laziest recruiter in the history of the United States Navy.

I told him I was twenty-eight. He barely looked up from his desk.

"You're basically at the cutoff for the Teams," he said flatly. "To even have a shot, you would have needed to be done with Basic Training *yesterday* and already have your scores locked in."

And he just left it at that.

He didn't pivot. He didn't try to sell me on a different path.

Here is the frustrating part: I was still well within the age range to join the regular Navy. I could have joined the Army. I could have joined the Air Force, like my brother Donnie. But this recruiter never mentioned a single alternative.

I walked out of that office believing I had aged out of the military entirely. I was ready to sign on the dotted line for any branch that day; it didn't have to be the SEALs anymore. I just wanted to serve.

But because of his apathy—and because I failed to do my own research to verify what he said—that boat sailed without me. Once again.

Now, let's dig a little deeper into these "What Ifs."

Sometimes, the heaviest questions aren't about careers or choices we made for ourselves. They are about the people who left our lives, or the people who were never allowed to enter them in the first place.

I grew up knowing who my father was, but he wasn't there; I only saw him every blue moon. The reality was complicated: he was already a married man when he met my mother. When she told him she was pregnant with me, he dropped a bombshell of his own—he had a wife.

My mother was faced with an impossible choice.

Option one: She could file for child support. This would force him to take responsibility, but it would almost certainly expose the affair to his wife and destroy his marriage.

Option two: She could keep his secret. This would protect his family, but it meant she would have to raise me alone, without his help.

She chose the second option.

That decision defined my childhood. It meant I grew up apart from my father and my siblings, while they grew up in a stable, two-parent household. If she had chosen differently—if she had exposed him—that marriage likely would have imploded. My siblings' lives would have been turned upside down by divorce and broken homes.

But here is the real kicker, the detail that makes the "What If" game so dangerous.

My dad had five children in total. Nate, Kisha, and Donnie came first. Then came me. And finally, after me, came my younger sister, Crystal.

Think about that timeline. If my mother had chosen to blow up his marriage back when she was pregnant with me, his life would have changed course completely. If that marriage had ended in divorce back then, there is a very strong possibility that my sister Crystal never would have been born.

Consider the position my dad was in: a married man, having a child with another woman. It would have been easy to hide.

But he didn't. I was still a secret, yes, but he showed up at the hospital. He signed the birth certificate. He was the one who named me Jason, and he made sure I carried his last name. He claimed me.

Years later, when we finally sat down and aired everything out, I was able to get a lifetime of questions off my chest. In that moment, we made a decision. We chose to move forward with love. We put the past behind us and focused entirely on building a relationship for the future.

And then... just as we started... he died.

Here is another heavy "What If"—one where a death directly paved the way for a birth.

My grandmother was my anchor. She was the reason I was surviving school, keeping me focused and on track. When she passed away in 1994, my world stopped. I shut down completely. I stopped caring, stopped working, and eventually, I stopped going.

Because of that emotional collapse, my mother made the hard decision to pull me out of the regular school system and send me to Job Corps.

That single move set off a chain reaction that defined my future.

Job Corps is where I met Wyvon.

Wyvon is the person who dragged me to the Black Family Reunion in 2001.

And that reunion is where I crossed paths with Shana—Talia's mother.

Trace the line backward.

If my grandmother hadn't died when she did, I likely would have stayed in school. I would have graduated the "normal" way. I never would have set foot in a Job Corps center. I never would have met Wyvon. I never would have been at that specific park on that specific day in 2001.

And Talia would not exist.

There is no timeline where my grandmother lives and my daughter Talia exists. The universe simply doesn't allow for both.

To have one, I had to lose the other. And that is the truly unfair part of life.

Then my mind drifts to my brother Kenny's father, Kenneth Jones Sr. What if he had lived?

The timeline of his life with us was tragically short. Kenneth Sr. married my mother in June of 1985. Fourteen months later, in August, their son—my brother, Kenneth "Kenny" Jones Jr.—was born. And just two months after that, in October, Kenneth Sr. was killed.

Sixteen months. That was the entire span of their family life.

Because of that sudden violence, my brother never got the chance to know his father. He never got to know that entire side of his bloodline.

Had Kenneth Sr. lived, everything would have looked different. Assuming he and my mom stayed together, Kenny and I would have likely grown up in a stable, two-parent household, just like our cousins.

And the ripple effects go even further. There was Jayson Jones, Kenneth Sr.'s other son. If his father had been alive, Jayson might have been a permanent fixture in our lives—a brother we grew up with. But when their dad died, that link was severed. Jayson moved back to Philly, and that was that.

You know the saying: *You have to play the hand you're dealt.*

It's a cliché for a reason. I've seen people start with a winning hand and still lose, just as I've seen people dealt a terrible hand somehow come out on top.

For the longest time, I was convinced I had been dealt a bad hand in life. But looking back, the truth is different. I was actually dealt a pretty good hand. It was just unique—a one-of-a-kind spread.

The problem wasn't the cards; it was the player. I didn't know how to play the game. I kept playing the wrong cards at the wrong times, making the game infinitely harder than it needed to be. I struggled for so long that, eventually, I tried to fold. I threw my hand in and gave up entirely.

People love to say that life unfolds exactly the way it is "supposed" to.

I remember challenging my dad on that once. I told him straight up, "That's bullshit."

My logic was cold and hard: I am only here because you had an affair. I am the byproduct of a mistake. Therefore, I am not *supposed* to be here.

But he didn't blink. He looked at me and assured me of one absolute truth.

"It doesn't matter how you got here," he said. "If you are here, you are supposed to be here."

That wisdom brings me to my wife, Torri.

We first crossed paths at Woodward High School. We even shared a mutual friend, yet somehow, we remained strangers passing in the halls. Unbeknownst to either of us, she stayed close to me throughout the years. We lived in the same neighborhoods, walked the same streets, and orbited the same circles from childhood all the way into adulthood.

We could have bumped into each other a thousand times. But we didn't.

Maybe we weren't ready. Maybe the versions of us that existed back then weren't meant to be together. We met exactly when we were supposed to. At the perfect time.

My daughter Natalie was born exactly one year after my father died. I named her in his honor—keeping a piece of Nathaniel alive in her.

Then came Jayla, who carries a piece of my own name.

Looking at them, I finally understood. It didn't matter how winding the path was. It didn't matter what cards I played or how many times I thought I was losing the game. Every single move up to this point was the right one.

Because *they* are here. And just as my father promised me—they are supposed to be here.

And they're only here because,

I never became a Navy Seal.

This book is a work of speculative memoir—a story born from the question that haunted me for twenty years: *"What if I became a Navy SEAL?"*

While the timeline of the bus crash and the coma served as the narrative vessel for this journey, the heart of this story is entirely true. The struggle for identity, the search for purpose, and the profound love I have for my wife, Torri, and our children are the absolute reality of my life.

The people named here are real. The places are real. And the gratitude I found in finally embracing my own life is the truest thing I know.

Sometimes, we have to imagine the life we lost to realize we already have the one we needed.

Jason Torri Lawrence Talia Natalie Jayla

www.ingramcontent.com/pod-product-compliance
Lightning Source LLC
Chambersburg PA
CBHW071758150726
47998CB00005B/1984